LEGO

NINJAGO™

Masters of Spinjitzu

GHOST NINJA

Story and art by Blue Ocean

LB
Little, Brown and Company
New York • Boston

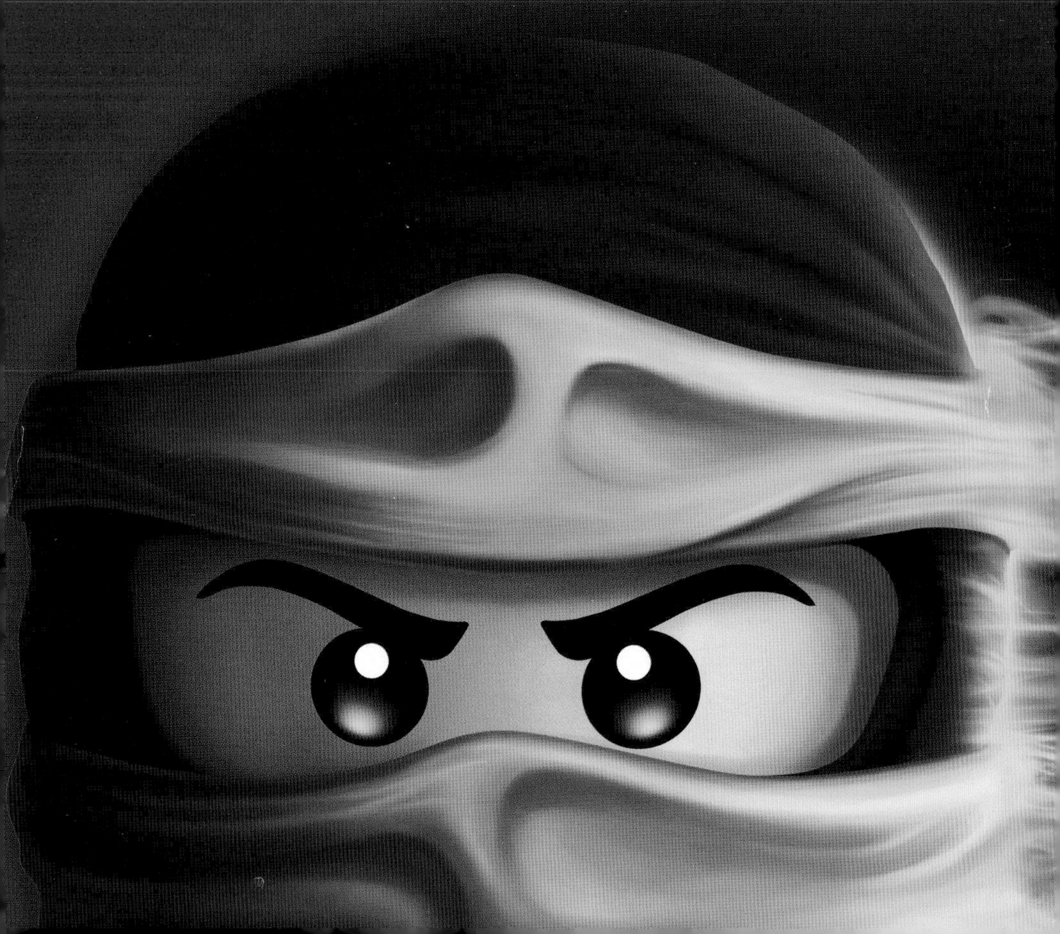

LEGO, the LEGO logo, the Brick and Knob configurations, the Minifigure,
NINJAGO and the NINJAGO logo are trademarks of the LEGO Group.

Produced by Little, Brown and Company under license
from the LEGO Group. © 2016 The LEGO Group

Comic artwork © 2016 by Blue Ocean Entertainment AG, Germany

Stories written by Christian Hector
Pencils by Jon Fernandez
Inks by Ivan Solans
Colors by Oriol San Julian & Javi Chaler

Little, Brown and Company

Hachette Book Group
1290 Avenue of the Americas, New York, NY 10104
Visit us at lb-kids.com

Little, Brown and Company is a division of Hachette Book Group, Inc.
The Little, Brown name and logo are trademarks
of Hachette Book Group, Inc.

The publisher is not responsible for websites (or their
content) that are not owned by the publisher.

First Edition: March 2016

Library of Congress Control Number: 2015960163

ISBN 978-0-316-30922-6 (paper over board) — ISBN 978-0-316-26611-6 (pb)

10 9 8 7 6 5 4 3 2 1

LAKE

Printed in the United States of America

LLOYD

Mourning the loss of his father, Lloyd fears change and how it might affect his future. His fragile state will allow the cursed spirit of Morro to possess his body and transform him into the most dangerous threat the ninja will have ever faced.

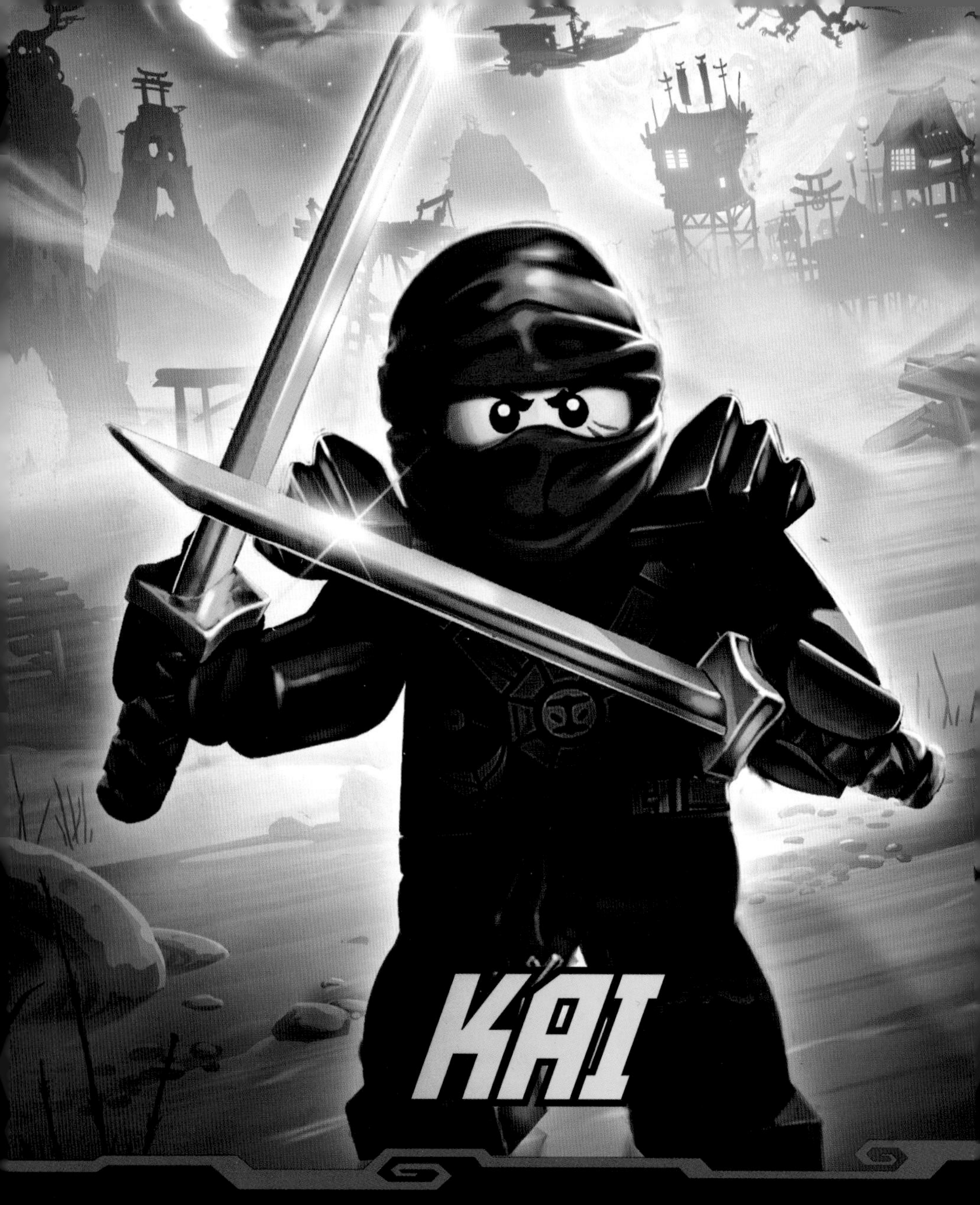
KAI

After promising Lloyd his protection, Kai feels personally obligated to single-handedly save him. But in order to get his friend back, he'll have to trust the team. In the end, Kai will learn that they all have weaknesses, but it's one another's strengths that will lift them up.

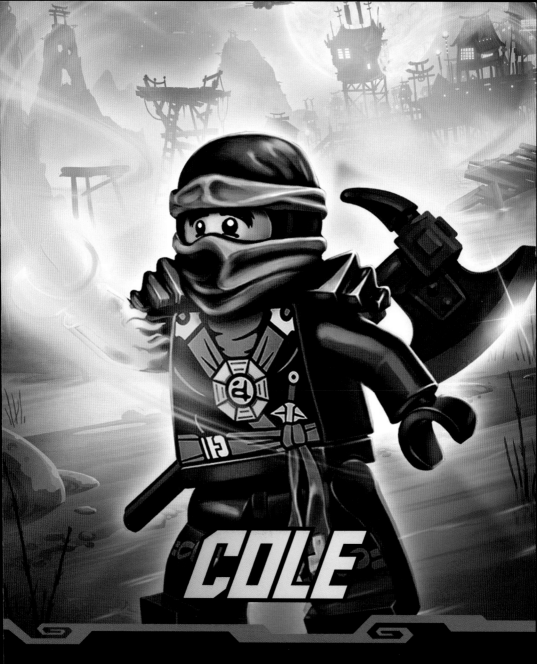

COLE

Cole may seem like a big fraidycat at times, but he always comes through for his friends. He starts this season off scared of ghosts, but when he gets trapped in a haunted house at sunrise, he's permanently changed into one. At first, everything seems bleak, but soon Cole will learn that with a new outlook come new opportunities and new abilities.

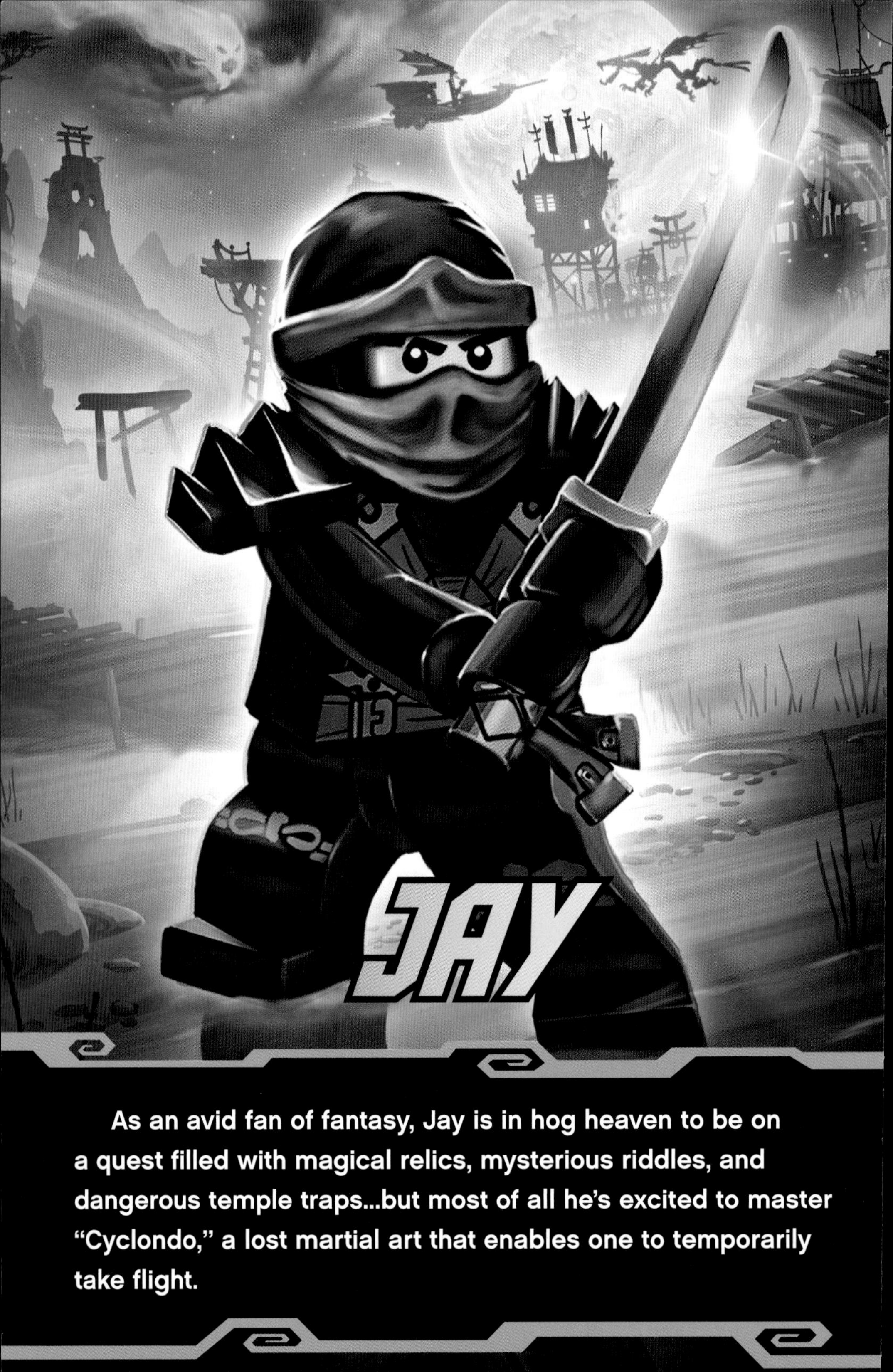
JAY

As an avid fan of fantasy, Jay is in hog heaven to be on a quest filled with magical relics, mysterious riddles, and dangerous temple traps...but most of all he's excited to master "Cyclondo," a lost martial art that enables one to temporarily take flight.

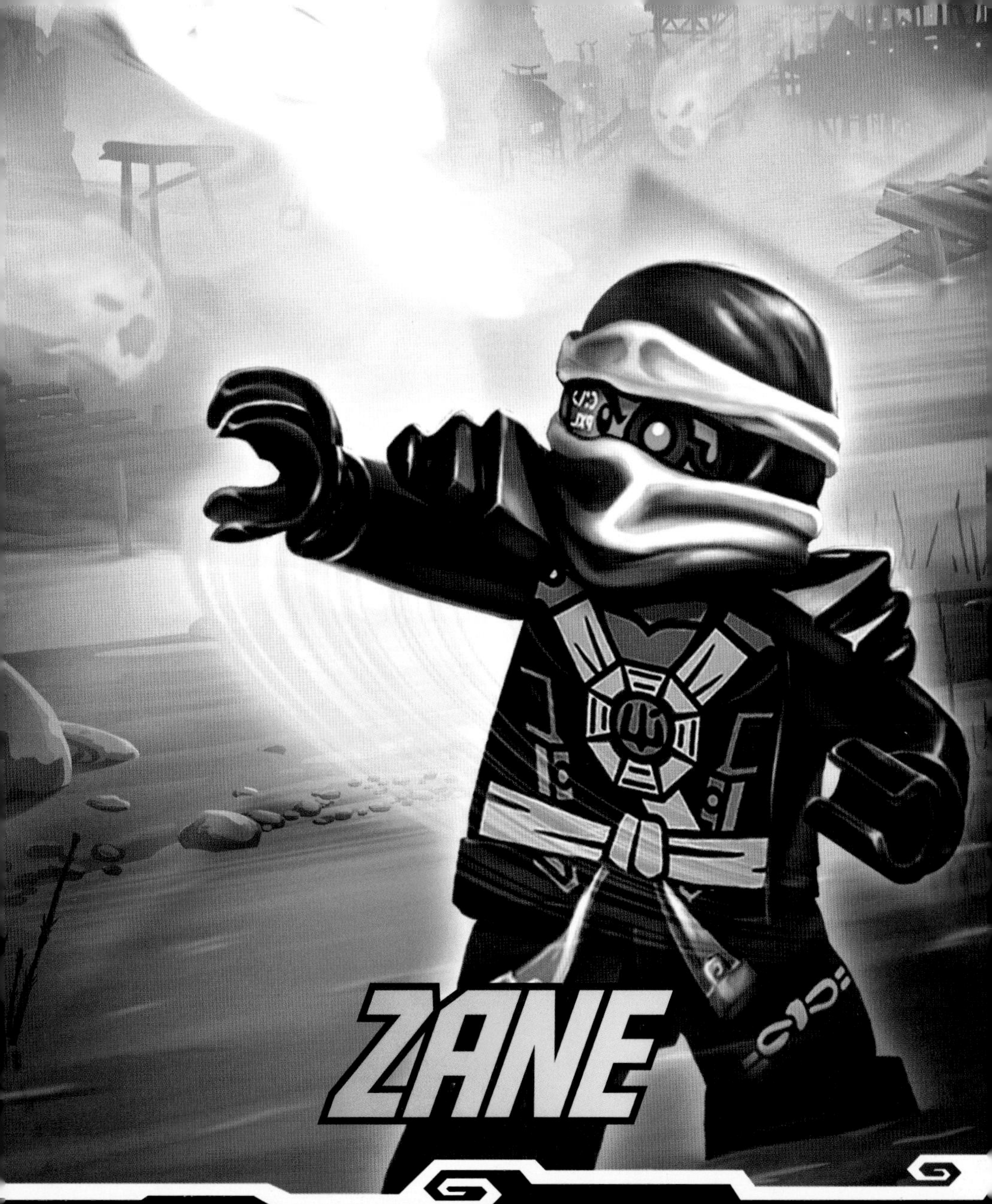
ZANE

Since Zane has already gone through his major transformation, he gladly takes a backseat for the rest of the ninja—but that doesn't mean he'll get lost in the fold. After a few wires get comically crossed in battle, he'll discover that he has a few more hidden dialects than he once thought.

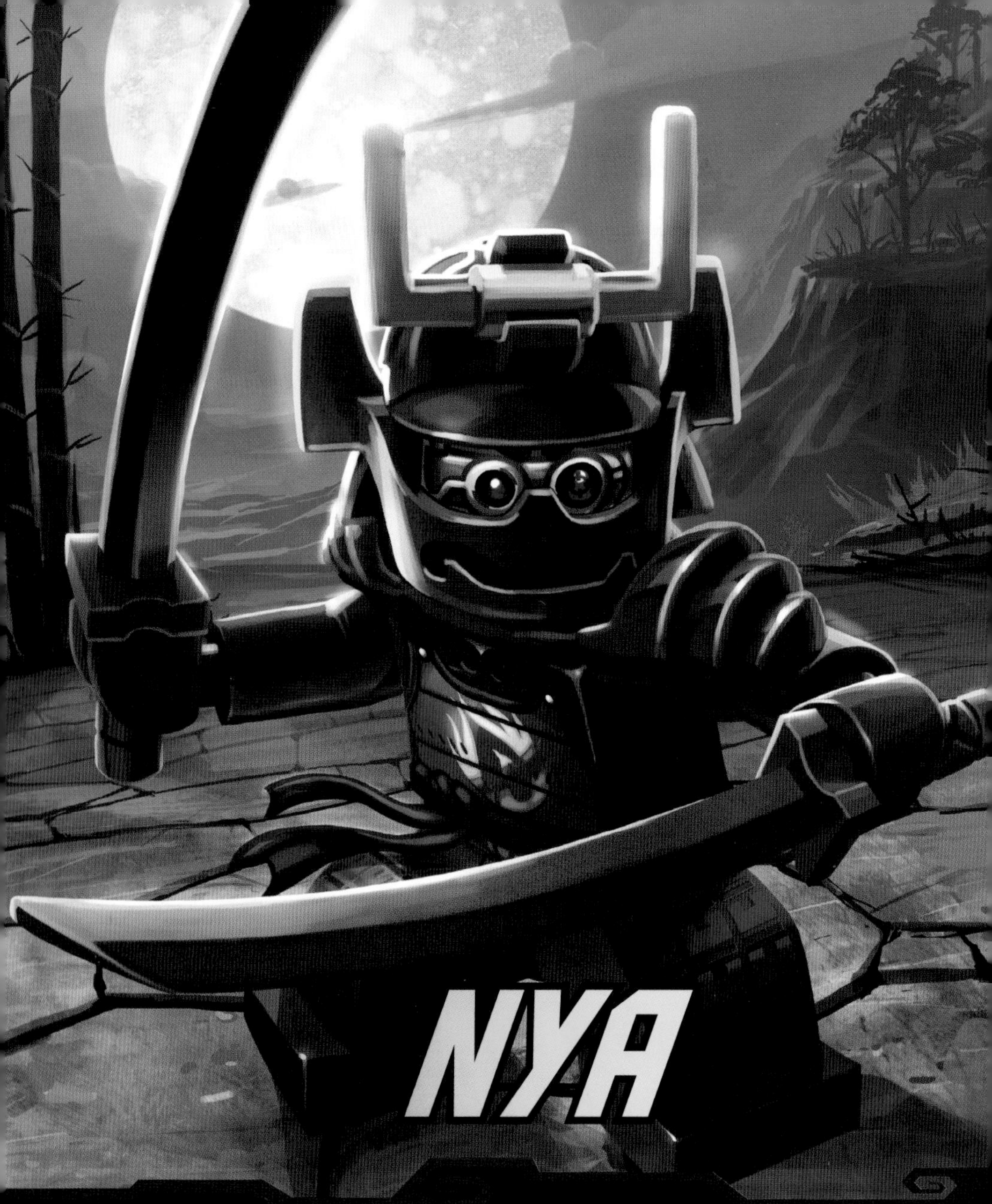

NYA

Besides Cole, no one goes through a bigger change than Nya. After being told she can't go on the quest, she learns she could become the most powerful weapon against the ghosts—as the Water Ninja. But does that mean she can't be Samurai X anymore? After her initial reluctance, she'll have to learn to go with the flow.

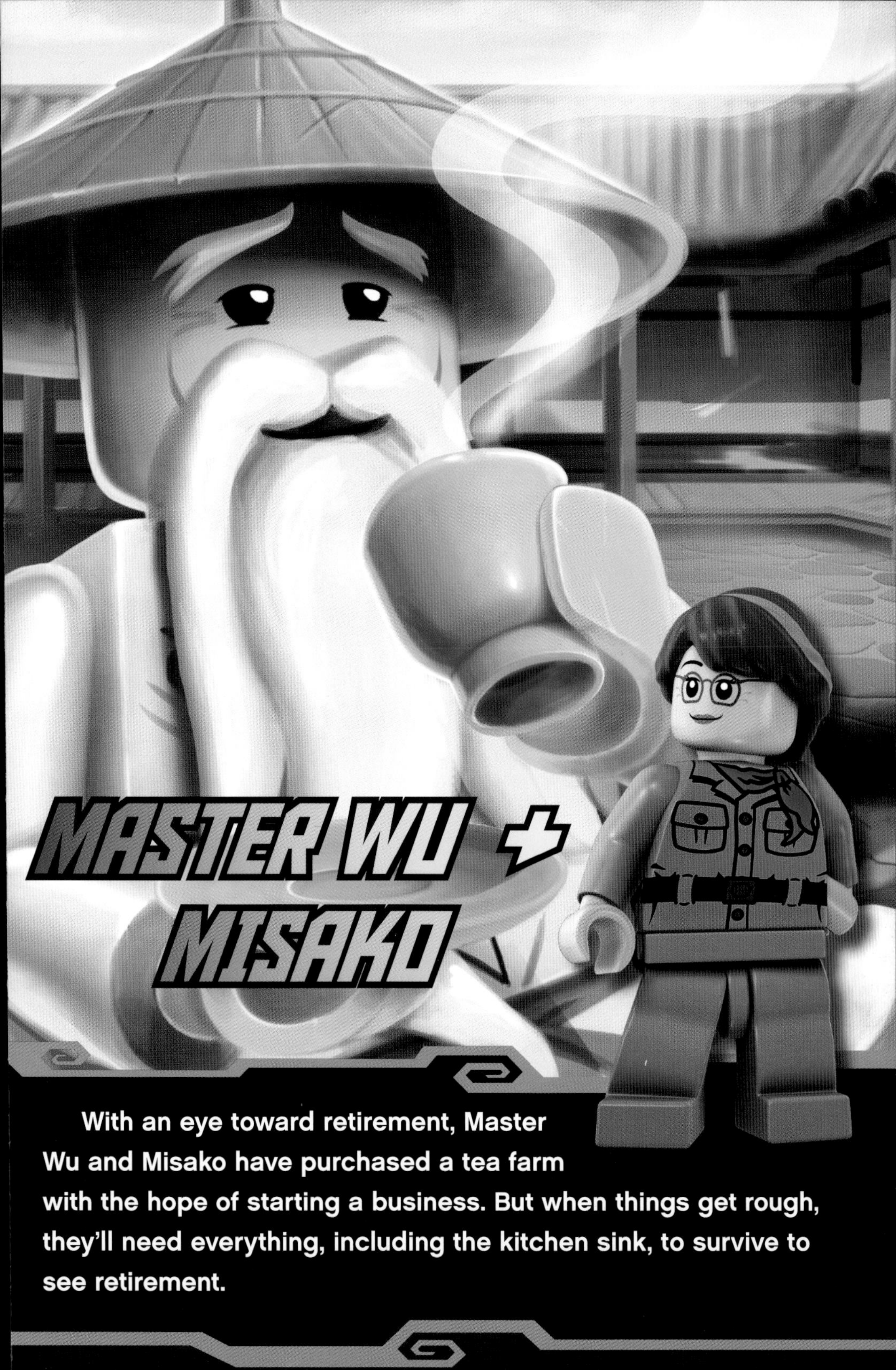

MASTER WU + MISAKO

With an eye toward retirement, Master Wu and Misako have purchased a tea farm with the hope of starting a business. But when things get rough, they'll need everything, including the kitchen sink, to survive to see retirement.

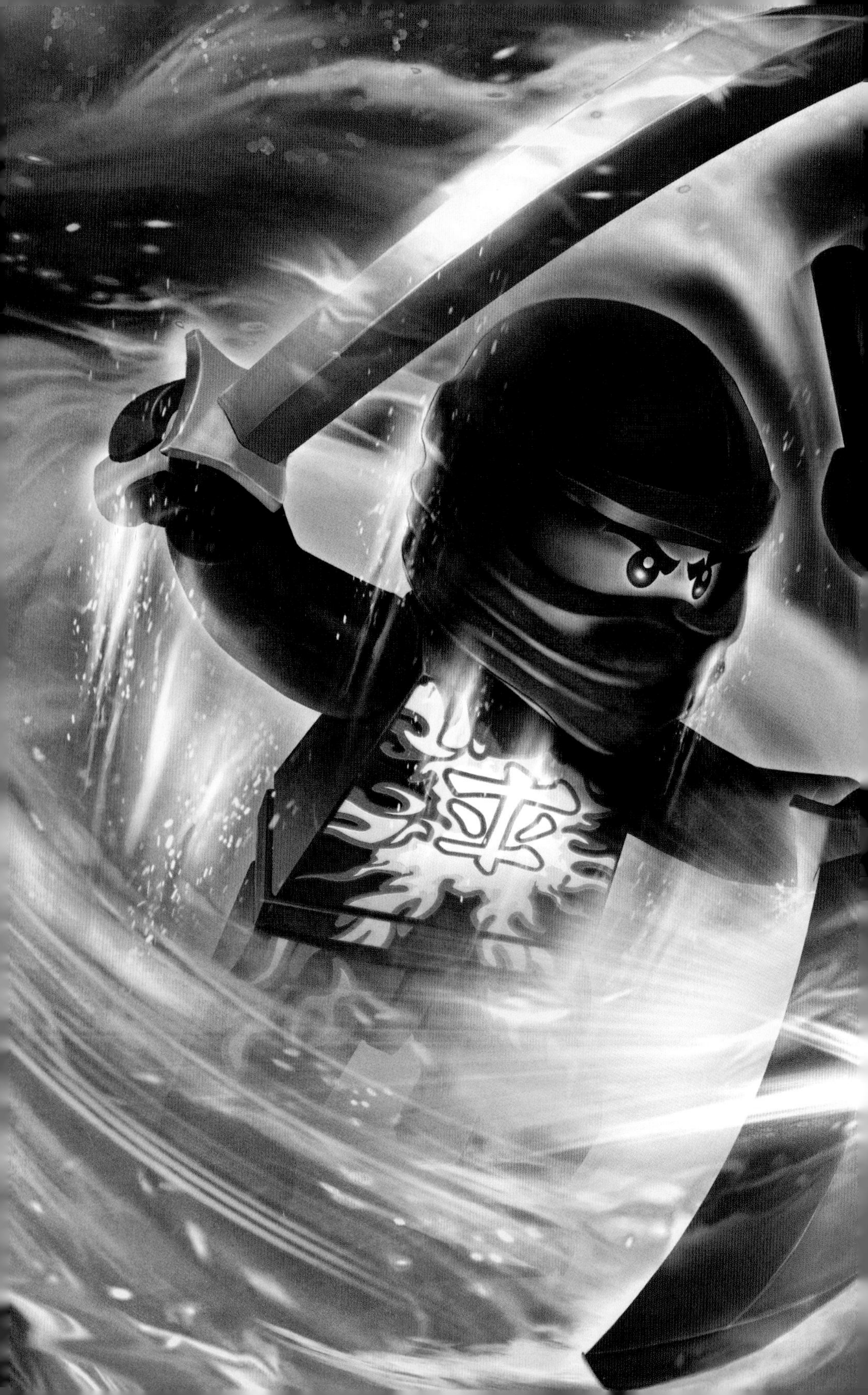

GHOST NINJA

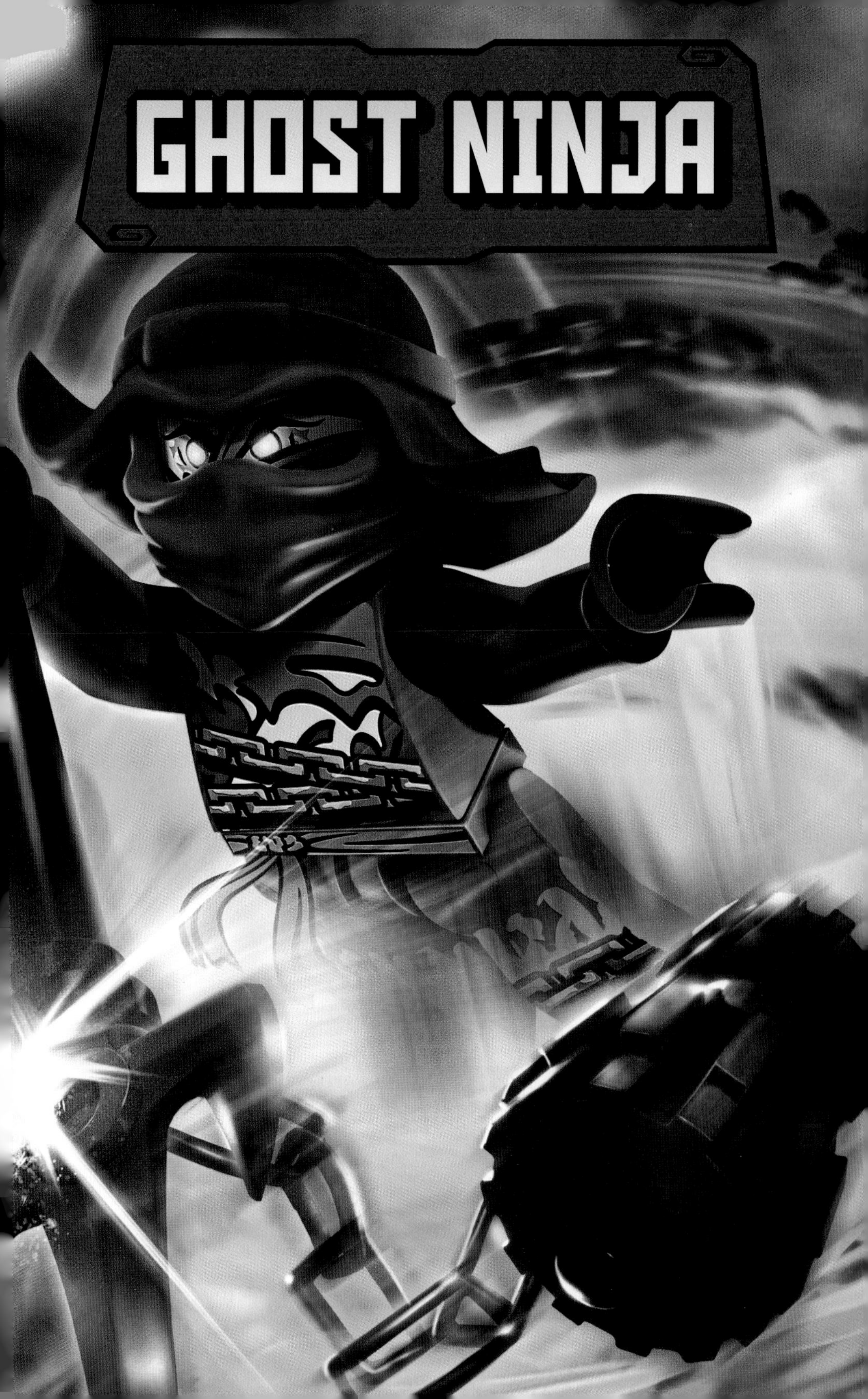

It is a Season of Change...

Since defeating Master Chen and his army in the Tournament of Elements, the ninja have never been more united. Yet Lloyd mourns the loss of his father to the Cursed Realm and questions his path ahead. Kai makes a solemn promise to look after Lloyd, as Nya looked after Kai upon their parents' demise. But that promise is put into jeopardy when a cold wind blows through Ninjago...

The cursed spirit of Morro—the Master of Wind, who also happens to be Master Wu's first pupil—possesses Lloyd. Now, without the aid of their elemental powers, the remaining ninja must square off against their brother, the Green Ninja. The good and the bad race to find the Lost Tomb of the First Spinjitzu Master, which holds a powerful relic called the Realm Crystal, which can not only affect Ninjago, but also other hidden realms the ninja have yet to discover...

THE NASTIEST OF THE NASTY!

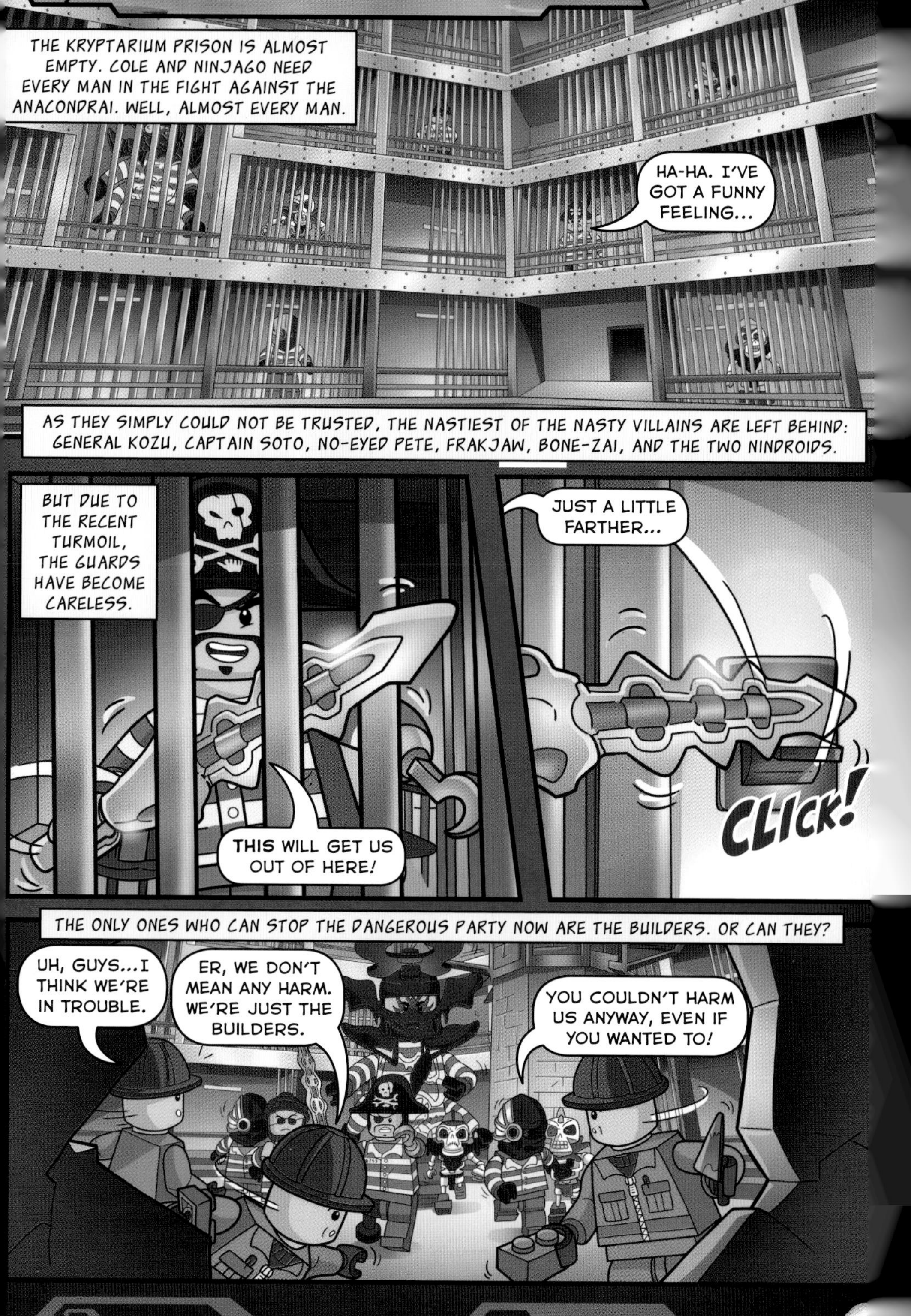

THE KRYPTARIUM PRISON IS ALMOST EMPTY. COLE AND NINJAGO NEED EVERY MAN IN THE FIGHT AGAINST THE ANACONDRAI. WELL, ALMOST EVERY MAN.
HA-HA. I'VE GOT A FUNNY FEELING...
AS THEY SIMPLY COULD NOT BE TRUSTED, THE NASTIEST OF THE NASTY VILLAINS ARE LEFT BEHIND: GENERAL KOZU, CAPTAIN SOTO, NO-EYED PETE, FRAKJAW, BONE-ZAI, AND THE TWO NINDROIDS.
BUT DUE TO THE RECENT TURMOIL, THE GUARDS HAVE BECOME CARELESS.
THIS WILL GET US OUT OF HERE!
JUST A LITTLE FARTHER...
CLICK!
THE ONLY ONES WHO CAN STOP THE DANGEROUS PARTY NOW ARE THE BUILDERS. OR CAN THEY?
UH, GUYS...I THINK WE'RE IN TROUBLE.
ER, WE DON'T MEAN ANY HARM. WE'RE JUST THE BUILDERS.
YOU COULDN'T HARM US ANYWAY, EVEN IF YOU WANTED TO!

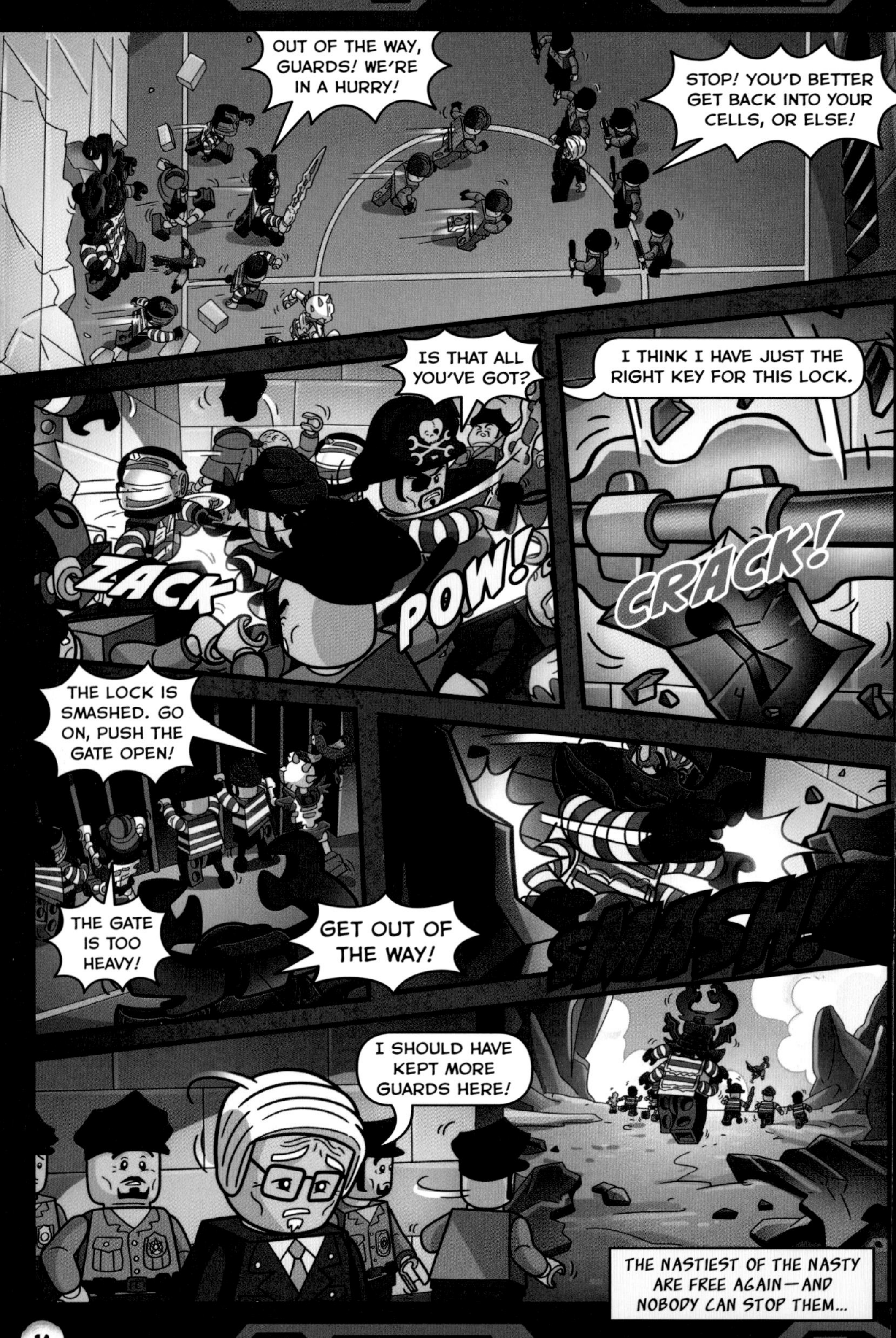
OUT OF THE WAY, GUARDS! WE'RE IN A HURRY!
STOP! YOU'D BETTER GET BACK INTO YOUR CELLS, OR ELSE!
IS THAT ALL YOU'VE GOT?
ZACK
POW!
I THINK I HAVE JUST THE RIGHT KEY FOR THIS LOCK.
CRACK!
THE LOCK IS SMASHED. GO ON, PUSH THE GATE OPEN!
THE GATE IS TOO HEAVY!
GET OUT OF THE WAY!
SMASH!
I SHOULD HAVE KEPT MORE GUARDS HERE!
THE NASTIEST OF THE NASTY ARE FREE AGAIN—AND NOBODY CAN STOP THEM...

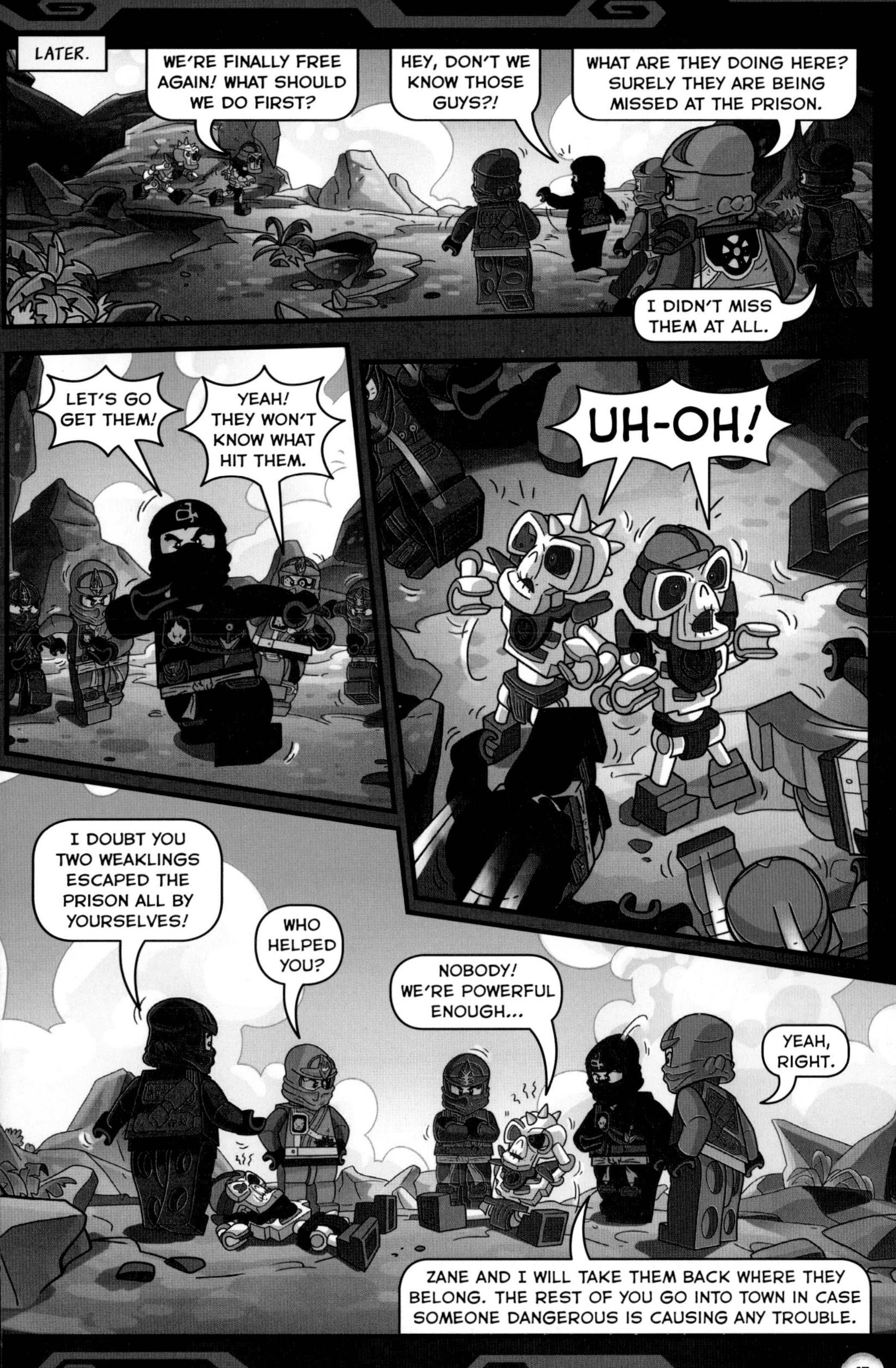
LATER.
WE'RE FINALLY FREE AGAIN! WHAT SHOULD WE DO FIRST?
HEY, DON'T WE KNOW THOSE GUYS?!
WHAT ARE THEY DOING HERE? SURELY THEY ARE BEING MISSED AT THE PRISON.
I DIDN'T MISS THEM AT ALL.
LET'S GO GET THEM!
YEAH! THEY WON'T KNOW WHAT HIT THEM.
UH-OH!
I DOUBT YOU TWO WEAKLINGS ESCAPED THE PRISON ALL BY YOURSELVES!
WHO HELPED YOU?
NOBODY! WE'RE POWERFUL ENOUGH...
YEAH, RIGHT.
ZANE AND I WILL TAKE THEM BACK WHERE THEY BELONG. THE REST OF YOU GO INTO TOWN IN CASE SOMEONE DANGEROUS IS CAUSING ANY TROUBLE.

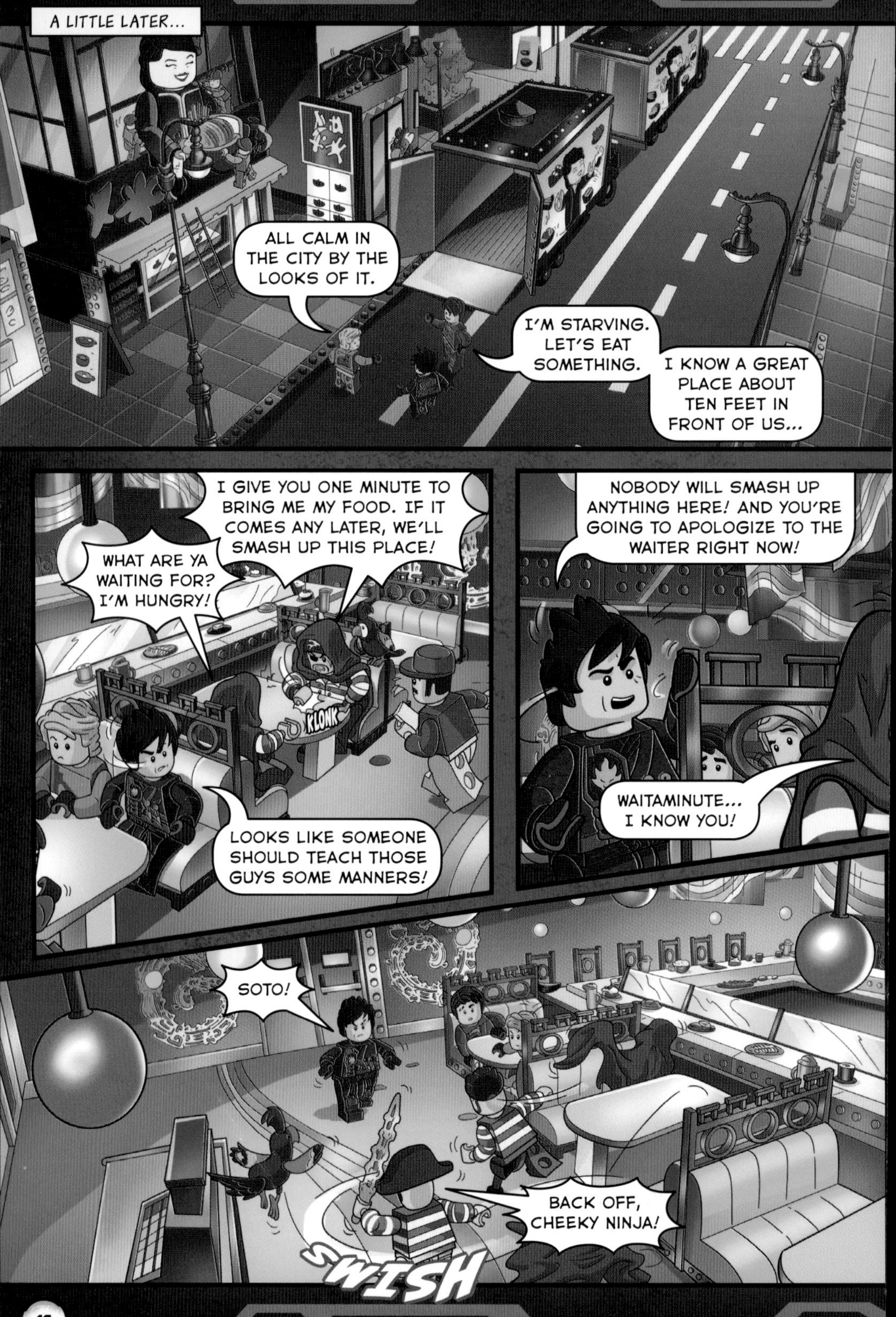

A LITTLE LATER...
ALL CALM IN THE CITY BY THE LOOKS OF IT.
I'M STARVING. LET'S EAT SOMETHING.
I KNOW A GREAT PLACE ABOUT TEN FEET IN FRONT OF US...
I GIVE YOU ONE MINUTE TO BRING ME MY FOOD. IF IT COMES ANY LATER, WE'LL SMASH UP THIS PLACE!
WHAT ARE YA WAITING FOR? I'M HUNGRY!
KLONK
LOOKS LIKE SOMEONE SHOULD TEACH THOSE GUYS SOME MANNERS!
NOBODY WILL SMASH UP ANYTHING HERE! AND YOU'RE GOING TO APOLOGIZE TO THE WAITER RIGHT NOW!
WAITAMINUTE... I KNOW YOU!
SOTO!
BACK OFF, CHEEKY NINJA!
SWISH

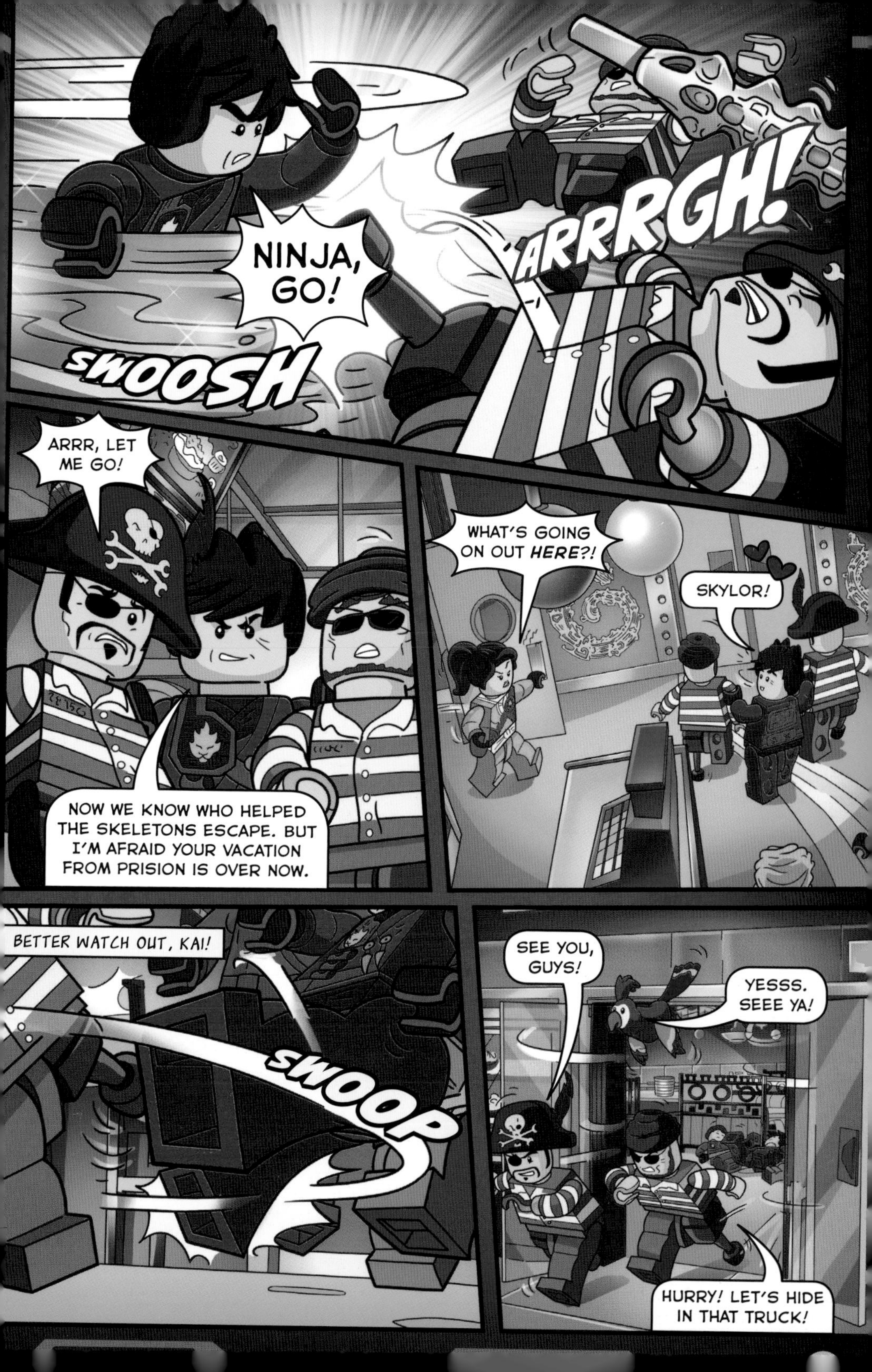
NINJA, GO!
ARRRGH!
SWOOSH
ARRR, LET ME GO!
NOW WE KNOW WHO HELPED THE SKELETONS ESCAPE. BUT I'M AFRAID YOUR VACATION FROM PRISION IS OVER NOW.
WHAT'S GOING ON OUT HERE?!
SKYLOR!
BETTER WATCH OUT, KAI!
SWOOP
SEE YOU, GUYS!
YESSS. SEEE YA!
HURRY! LET'S HIDE IN THAT TRUCK!

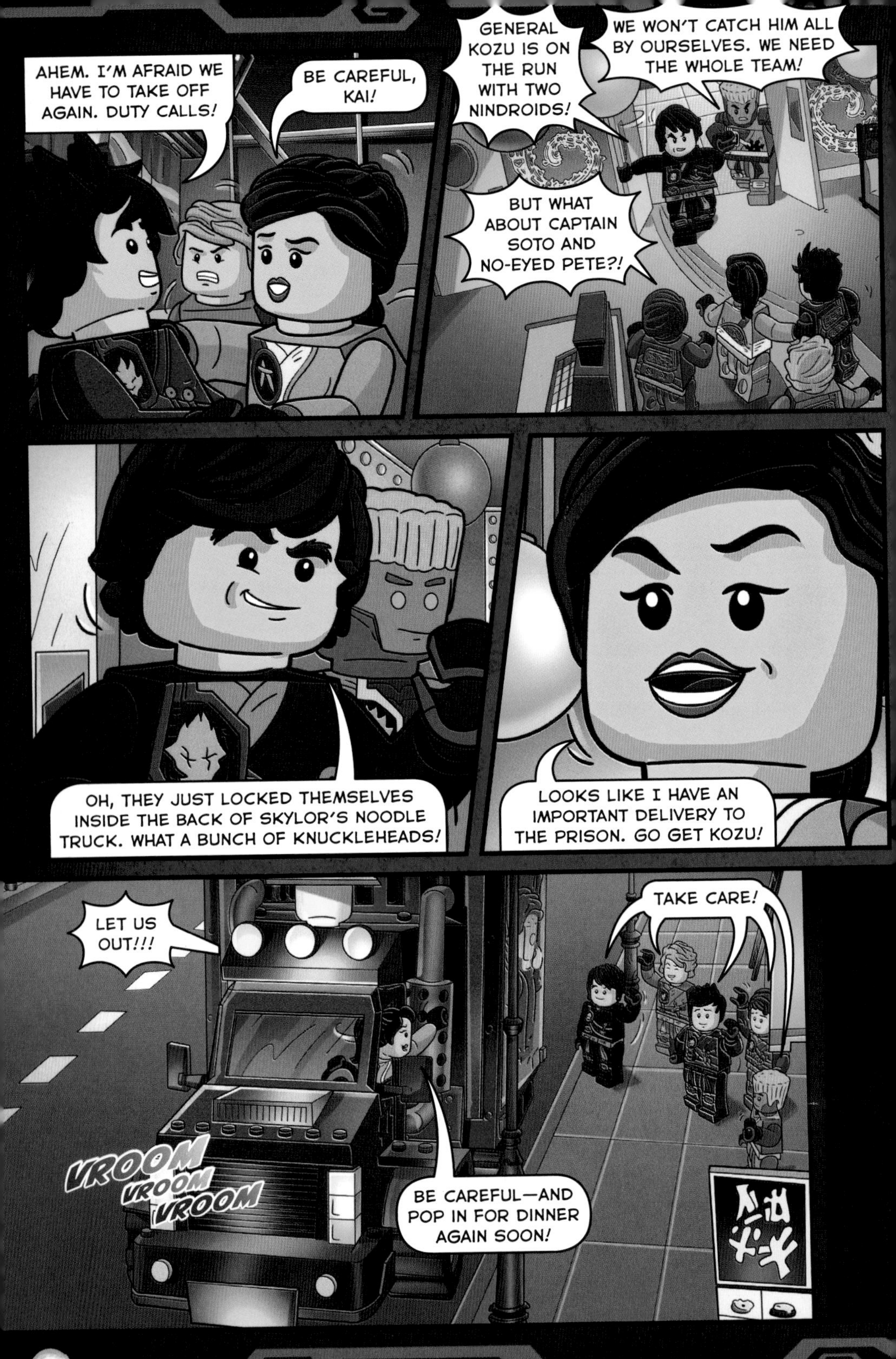
AHEM. I'M AFRAID WE HAVE TO TAKE OFF AGAIN. DUTY CALLS!
BE CAREFUL, KAI!
GENERAL KOZU IS ON THE RUN WITH TWO NINDROIDS!
WE WON'T CATCH HIM ALL BY OURSELVES. WE NEED THE WHOLE TEAM!
BUT WHAT ABOUT CAPTAIN SOTO AND NO-EYED PETE?!
OH, THEY JUST LOCKED THEMSELVES INSIDE THE BACK OF SKYLOR'S NOODLE TRUCK. WHAT A BUNCH OF KNUCKLEHEADS!
LOOKS LIKE I HAVE AN IMPORTANT DELIVERY TO THE PRISON. GO GET KOZU!
LET US OUT!!!
TAKE CARE!
VROOM VROOM VROOM
BE CAREFUL—AND POP IN FOR DINNER AGAIN SOON!

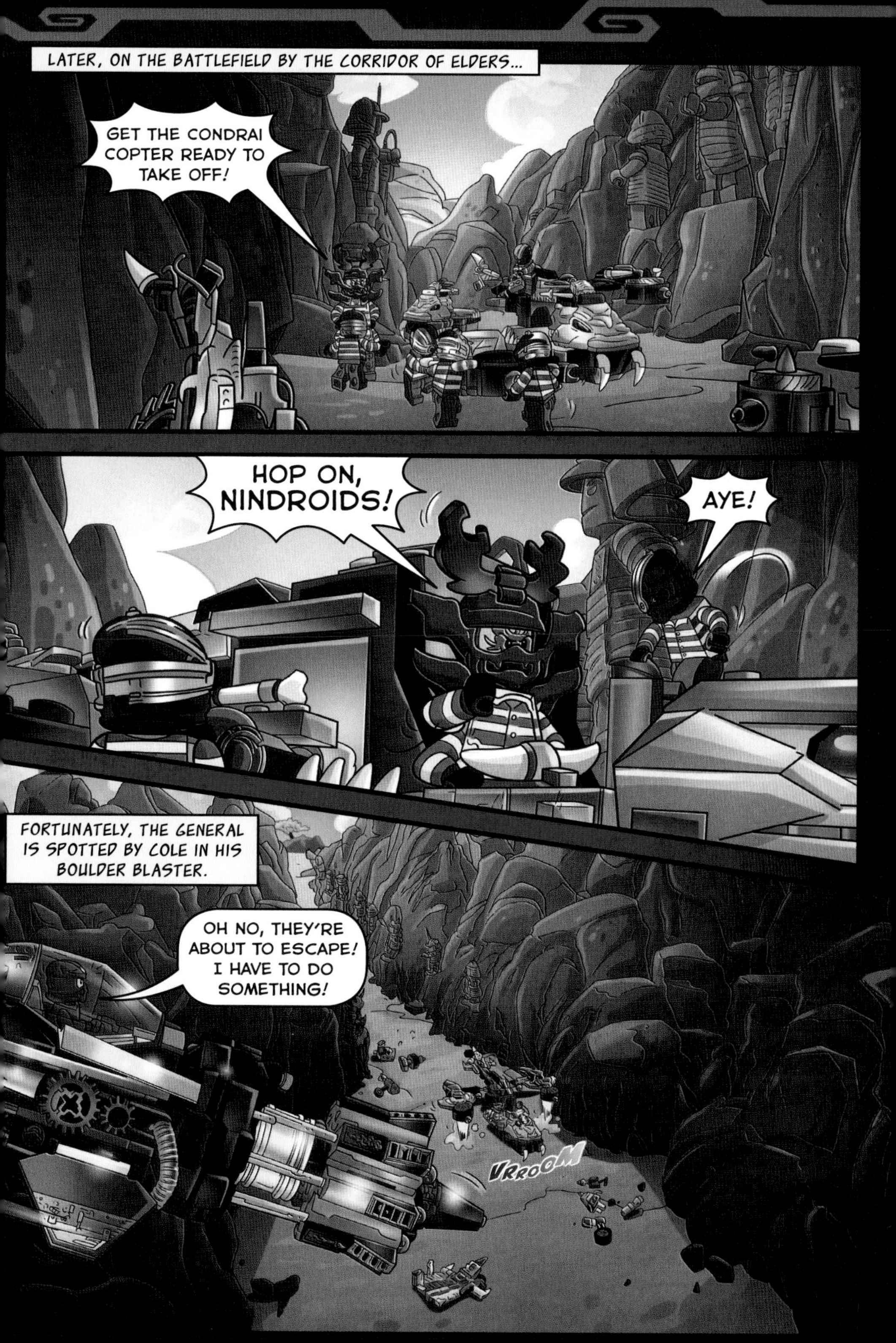
LATER, ON THE BATTLEFIELD BY THE CORRIDOR OF ELDERS...
GET THE CONDRAI COPTER READY TO TAKE OFF!
HOP ON, NINDROIDS!
AYE!
FORTUNATELY, THE GENERAL IS SPOTTED BY COLE IN HIS BOULDER BLASTER.
OH NO, THEY'RE ABOUT TO ESCAPE! I HAVE TO DO SOMETHING!
VRROOM

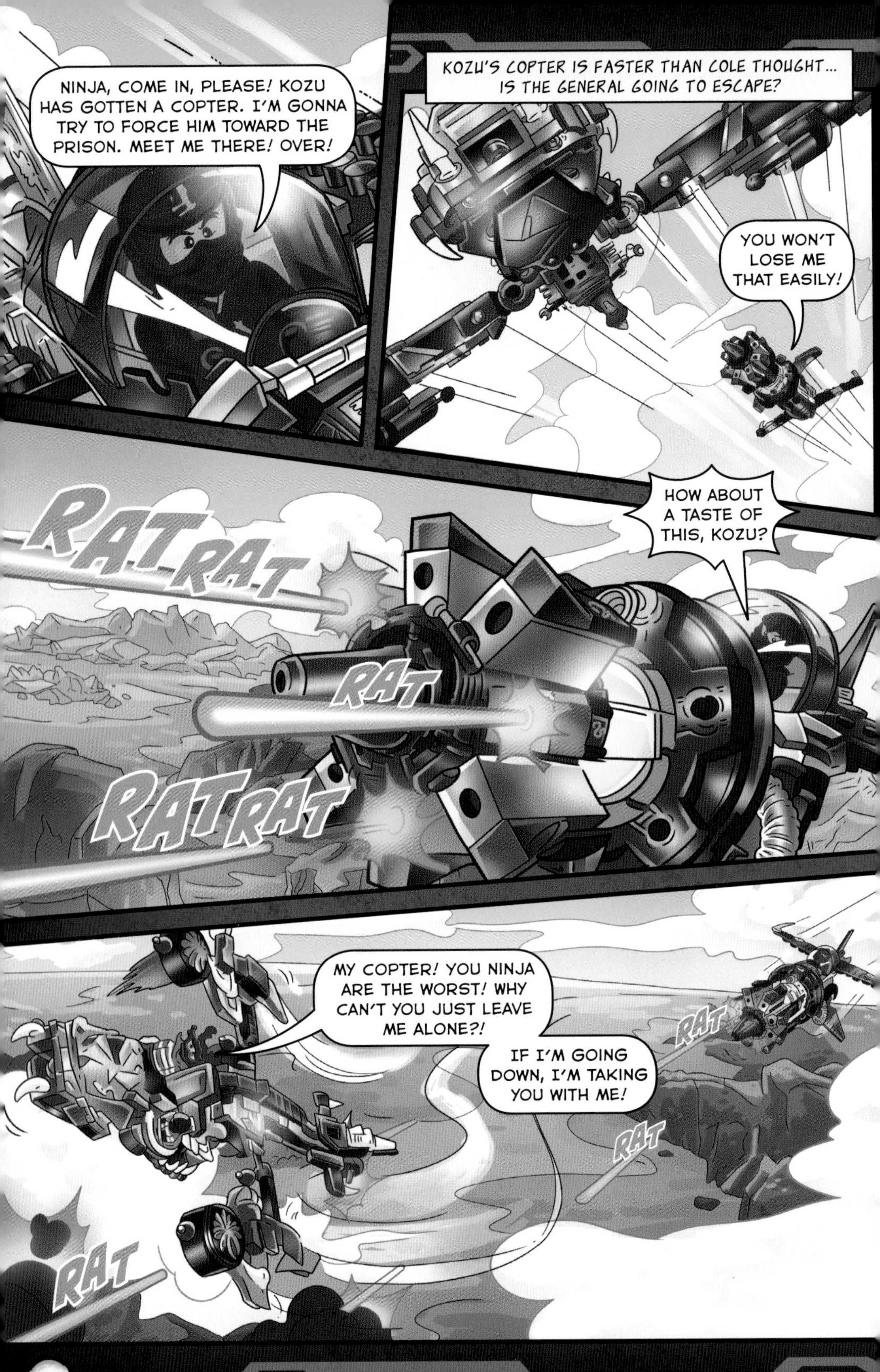
NINJA, COME IN, PLEASE! KOZU HAS GOTTEN A COPTER. I'M GONNA TRY TO FORCE HIM TOWARD THE PRISON. MEET ME THERE! OVER!
KOZU'S COPTER IS FASTER THAN COLE THOUGHT... IS THE GENERAL GOING TO ESCAPE?
YOU WON'T LOSE ME THAT EASILY!
RATRATRAT
HOW ABOUT A TASTE OF THIS, KOZU?
RAT
RATRATRAT
MY COPTER! YOU NINJA ARE THE WORST! WHY CAN'T YOU JUST LEAVE ME ALONE?!
IF I'M GOING DOWN, I'M TAKING YOU WITH ME!
RAT
RAT
RAT

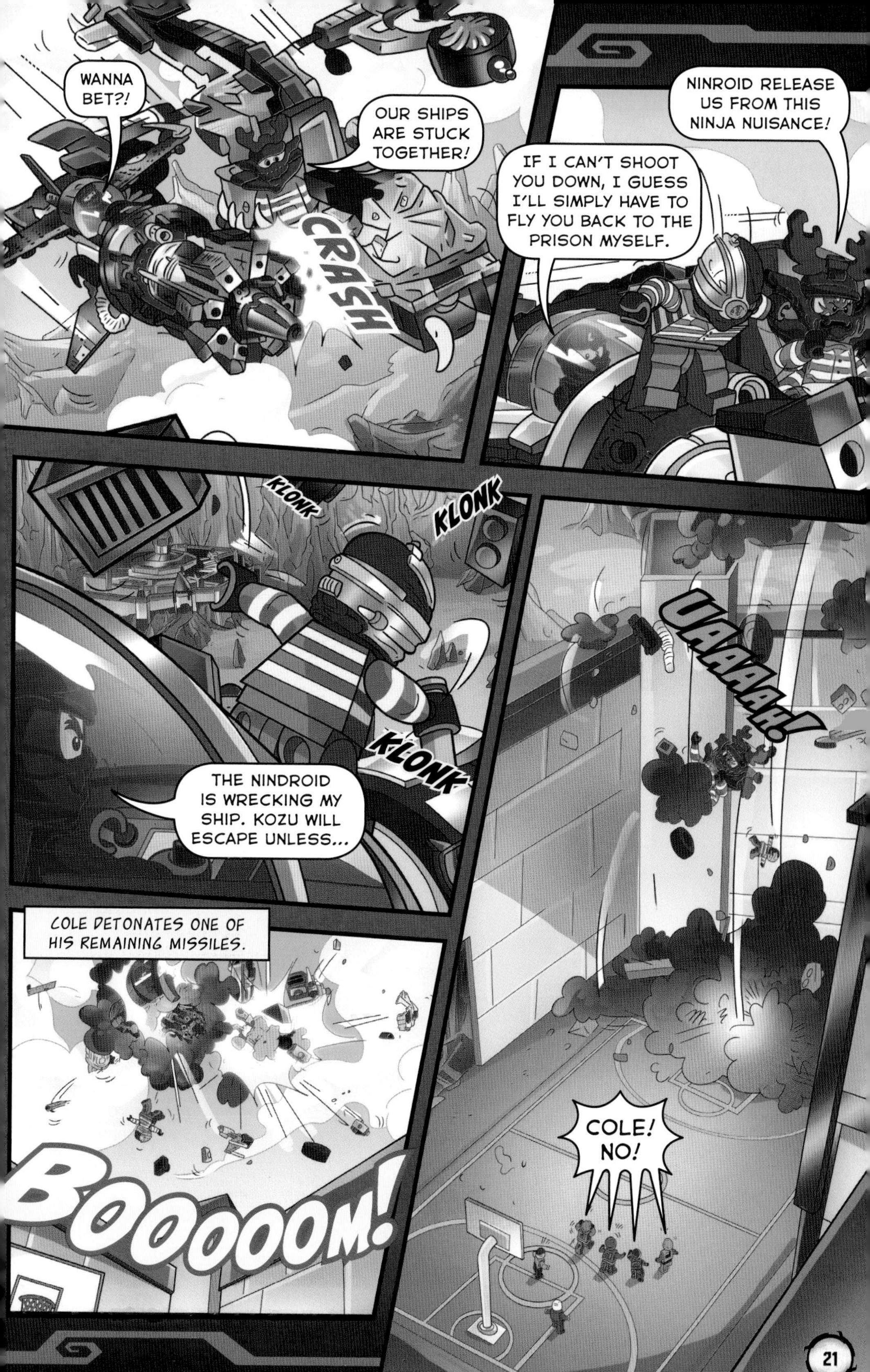
WANNA BET?!
OUR SHIPS ARE STUCK TOGETHER!
CRASH
NINROID RELEASE US FROM THIS NINJA NUISANCE!
IF I CAN'T SHOOT YOU DOWN, I GUESS I'LL SIMPLY HAVE TO FLY YOU BACK TO THE PRISON MYSELF.
KLONK
KLONK
KLONK
THE NINDROID IS WRECKING MY SHIP. KOZU WILL ESCAPE UNLESS...
UAAAAH!
COLE DETONATES ONE OF HIS REMAINING MISSILES.
BOOOOOM!
COLE! NO!

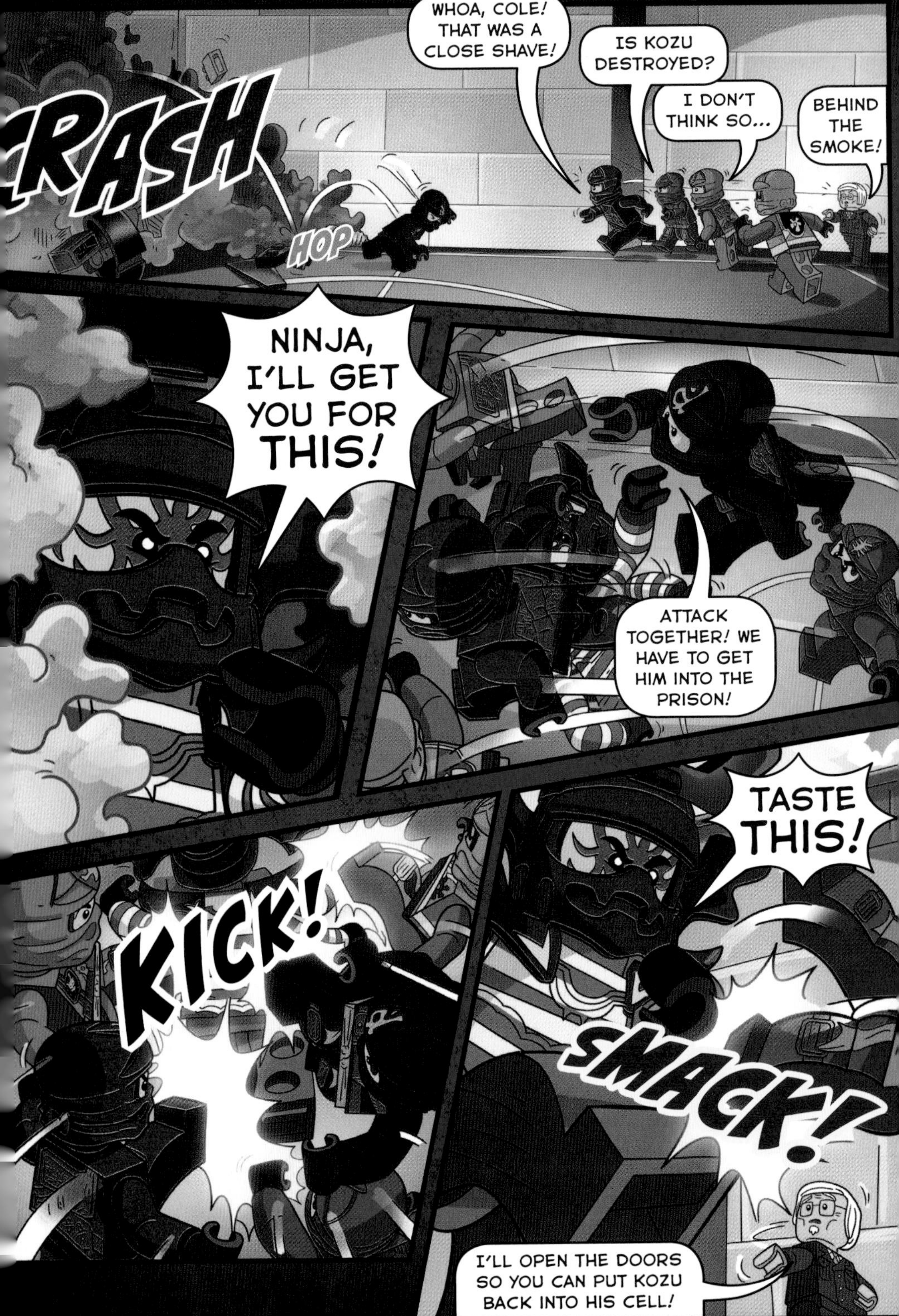

RASH
HOP
WHOA, COLE! THAT WAS A CLOSE SHAVE!
IS KOZU DESTROYED?
I DON'T THINK SO...
BEHIND THE SMOKE!
NINJA, I'LL GET YOU FOR THIS!
ATTACK TOGETHER! WE HAVE TO GET HIM INTO THE PRISON!
KICK!
TASTE THIS!
SMACK!
I'LL OPEN THE DOORS SO YOU CAN PUT KOZU BACK INTO HIS CELL!

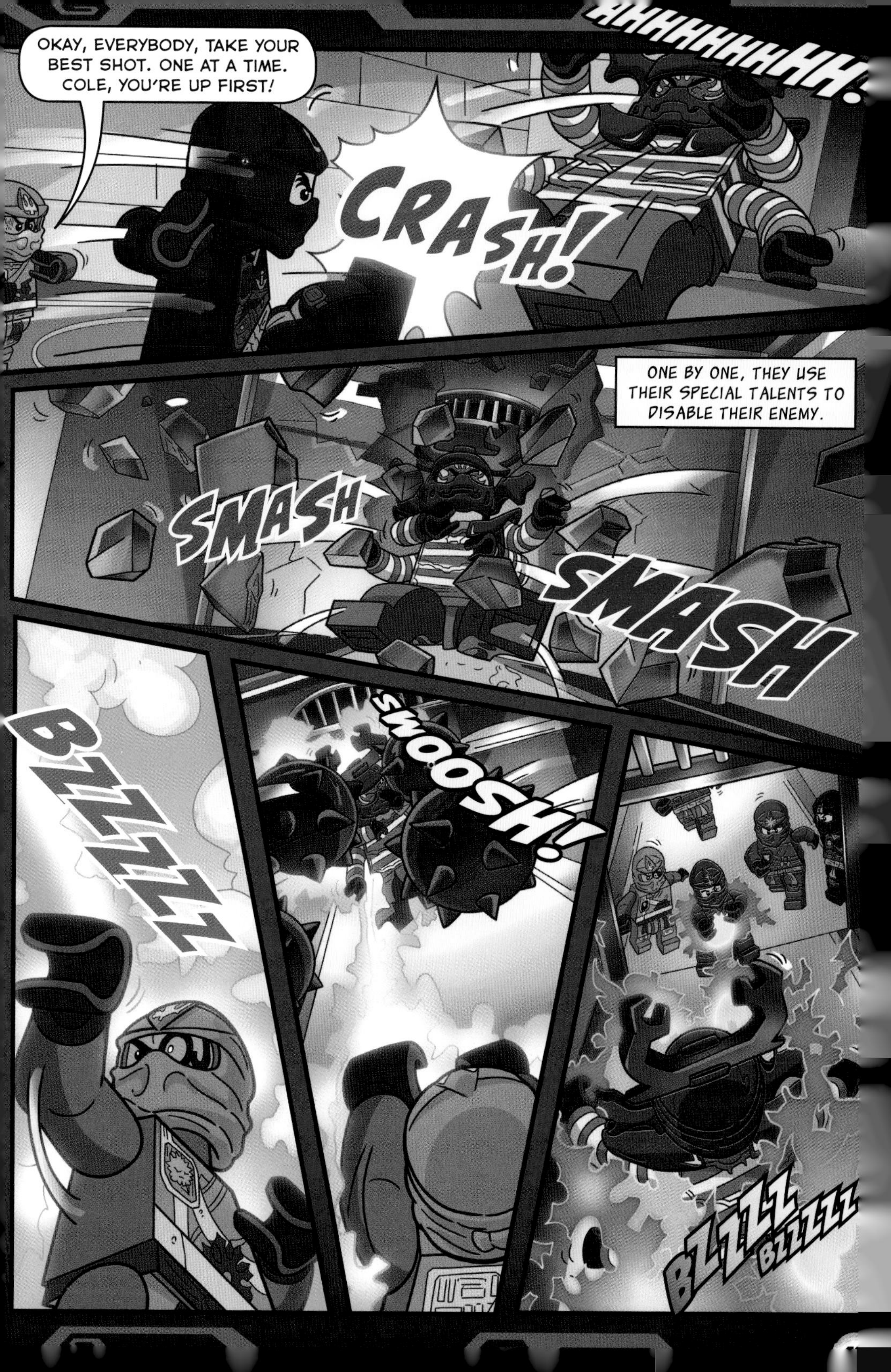
OKAY, EVERYBODY, TAKE YOUR BEST SHOT. ONE AT A TIME. COLE, YOU'RE UP FIRST!
AHHHHHHHHH!
CRASH!
ONE BY ONE, THEY USE THEIR SPECIAL TALENTS TO DISABLE THEIR ENEMY.
SMASH
SMASH
BZZZZZ
SWOOSH!
BZZZZ
BZZZZZ

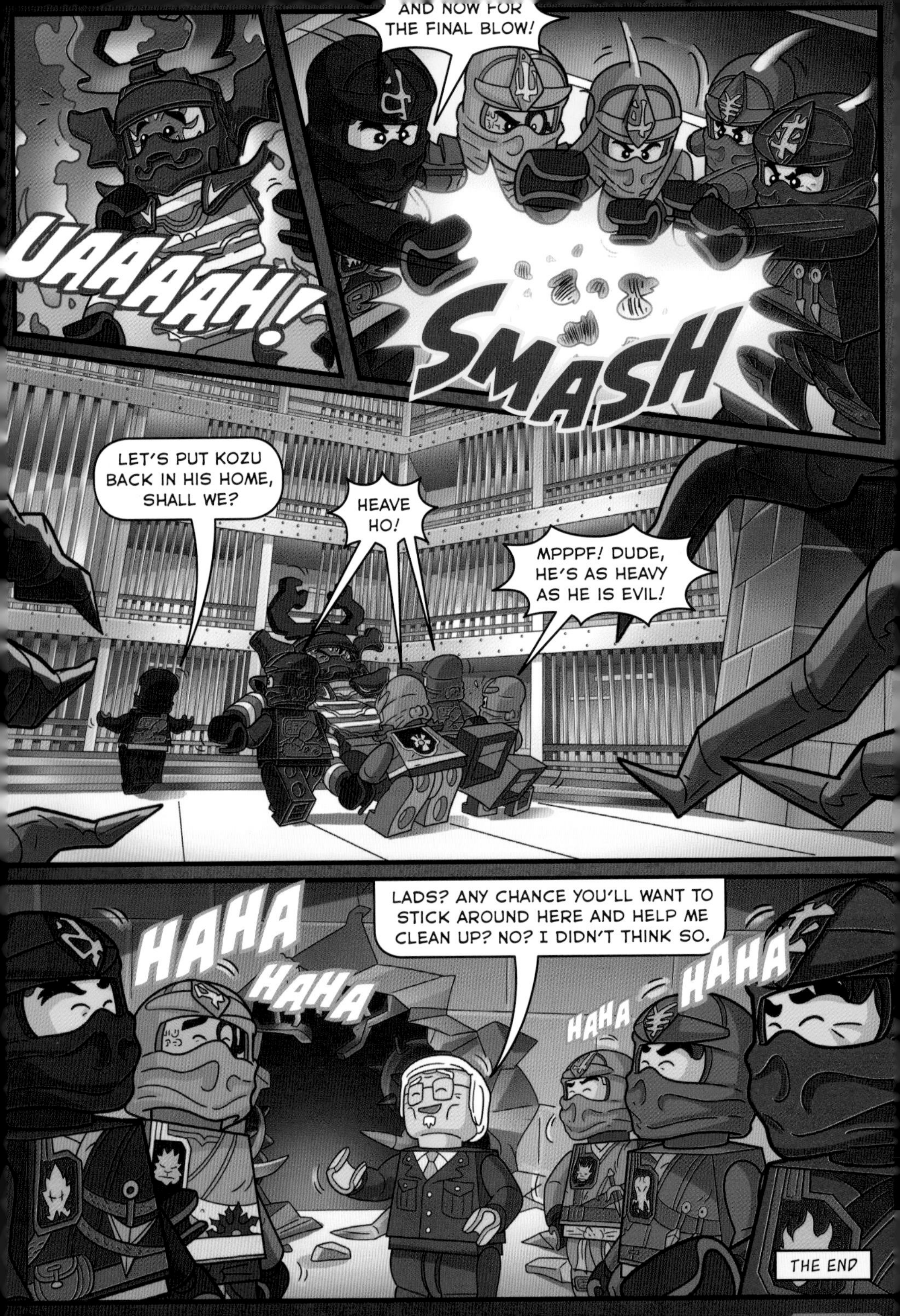
AND NOW FOR THE FINAL BLOW!
UAAAAAH!
SMASH
LET'S PUT KOZU BACK IN HIS HOME, SHALL WE?
HEAVE HO!
MPPPF! DUDE, HE'S AS HEAVY AS HE IS EVIL!
HAHA
HAHA
LADS? ANY CHANCE YOU'LL WANT TO STICK AROUND HERE AND HELP ME CLEAN UP? NO? I DIDN'T THINK SO.
HAHA
HAHA
THE END

NINJA IN DREAMLAND

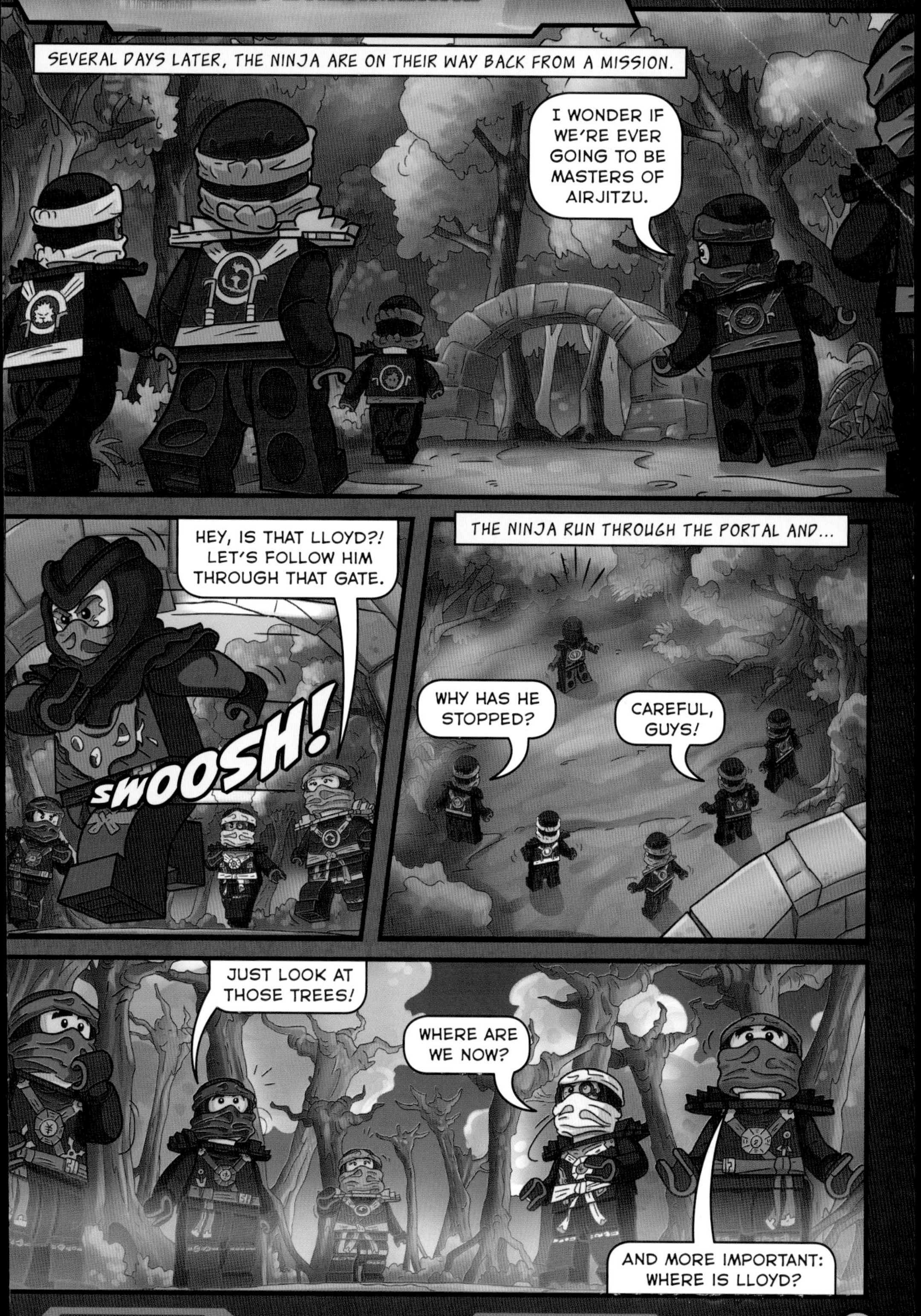

SEVERAL DAYS LATER, THE NINJA ARE ON THEIR WAY BACK FROM A MISSION.
I WONDER IF WE'RE EVER GOING TO BE MASTERS OF AIRJITZU.
HEY, IS THAT LLOYD?! LET'S FOLLOW HIM THROUGH THAT GATE.
SWOOSH!
THE NINJA RUN THROUGH THE PORTAL AND...
WHY HAS HE STOPPED?
CAREFUL, GUYS!
JUST LOOK AT THOSE TREES!
WHERE ARE WE NOW?
AND MORE IMPORTANT: WHERE IS LLOYD?

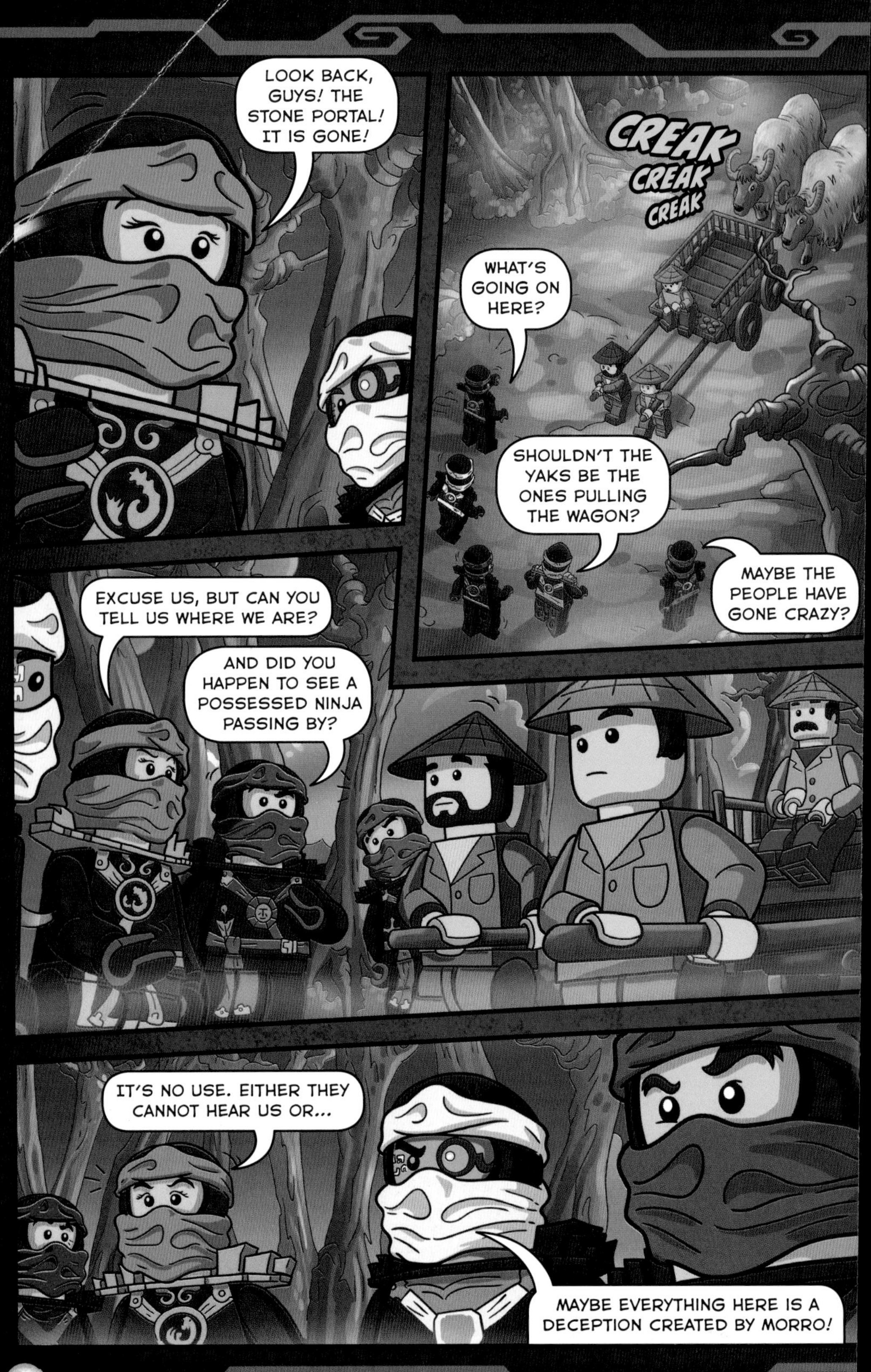
LOOK BACK, GUYS! THE STONE PORTAL! IT IS GONE!
CREAK
CREAK
CREAK
WHAT'S GOING ON HERE?
SHOULDN'T THE YAKS BE THE ONES PULLING THE WAGON?
MAYBE THE PEOPLE HAVE GONE CRAZY?
EXCUSE US, BUT CAN YOU TELL US WHERE WE ARE?
AND DID YOU HAPPEN TO SEE A POSSESSED NINJA PASSING BY?
IT'S NO USE. EITHER THEY CANNOT HEAR US OR...
MAYBE EVERYTHING HERE IS A DECEPTION CREATED BY MORRO!

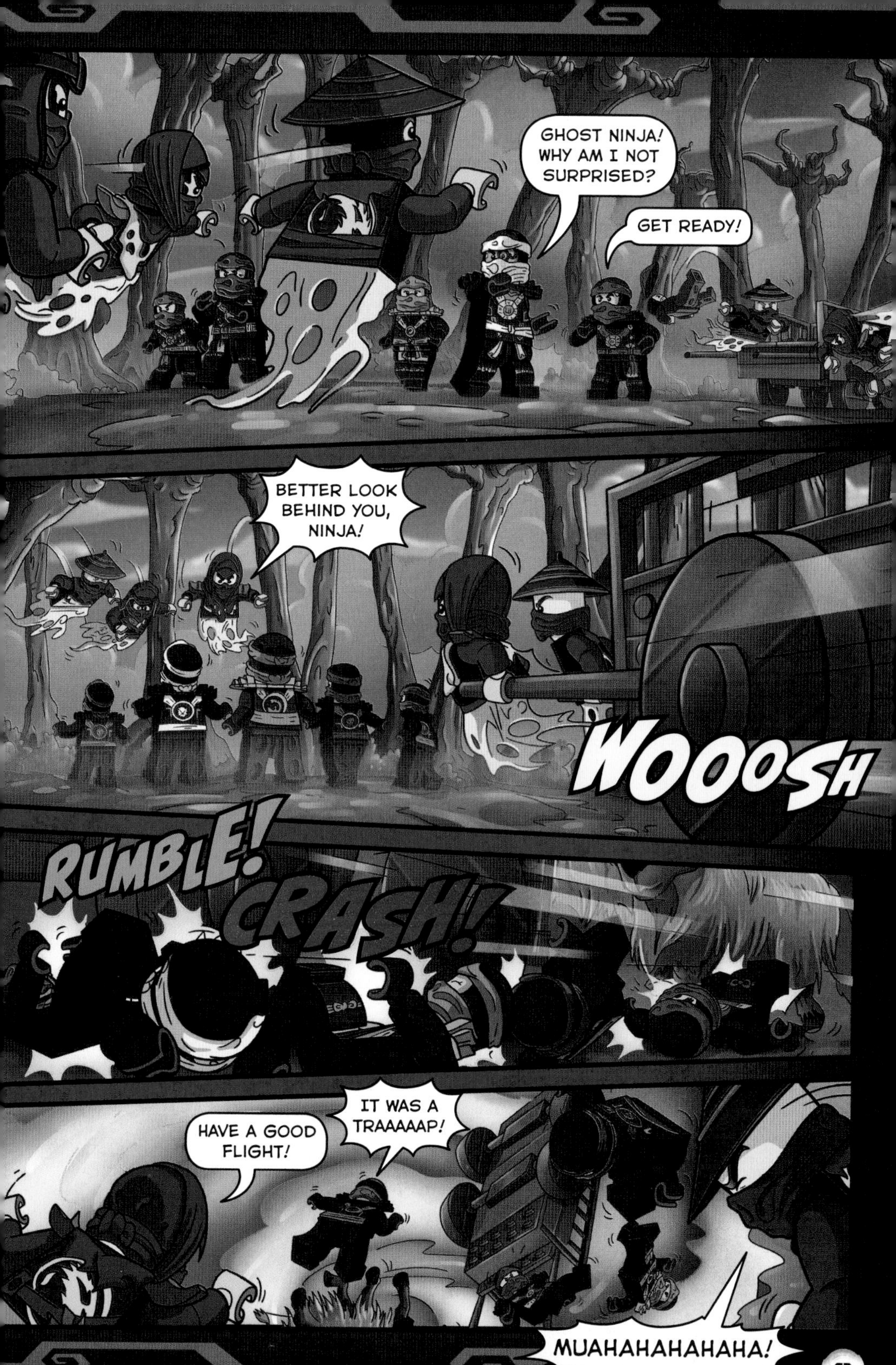
GHOST NINJA! WHY AM I NOT SURPRISED?
GET READY!
BETTER LOOK BEHIND YOU, NINJA!
WOOOSH
RUMBLE!
CRASH!
HAVE A GOOD FLIGHT!
IT WAS A TRAAAAAP!
MUAHAHAHAHAHA!

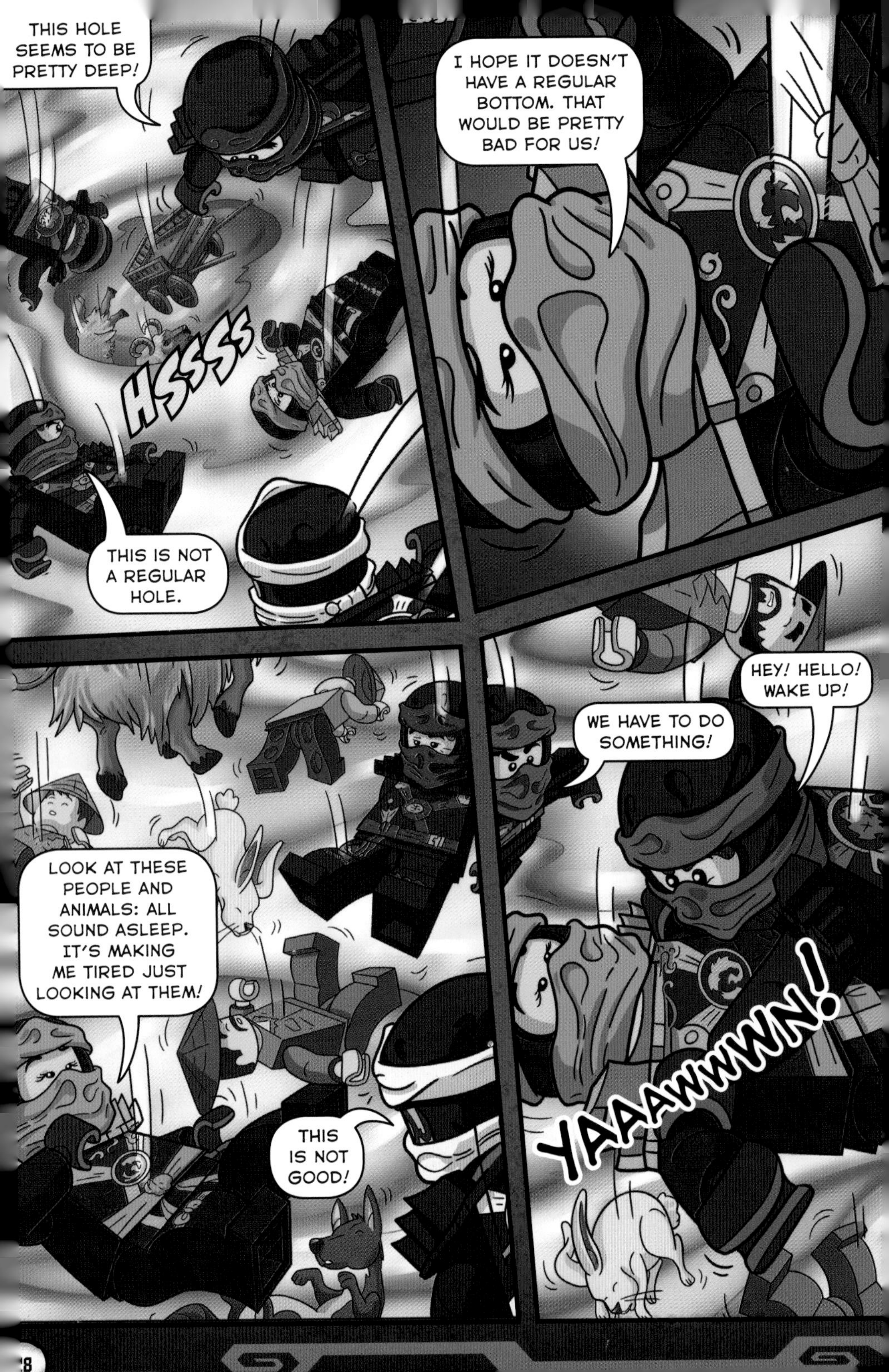
THIS HOLE SEEMS TO BE PRETTY DEEP!
HSSSS
THIS IS NOT A REGULAR HOLE.
I HOPE IT DOESN'T HAVE A REGULAR BOTTOM. THAT WOULD BE PRETTY BAD FOR US!
LOOK AT THESE PEOPLE AND ANIMALS: ALL SOUND ASLEEP. IT'S MAKING ME TIRED JUST LOOKING AT THEM!
THIS IS NOT GOOD!
WE HAVE TO DO SOMETHING!
HEY! HELLO! WAKE UP!
YAAAWWWN!

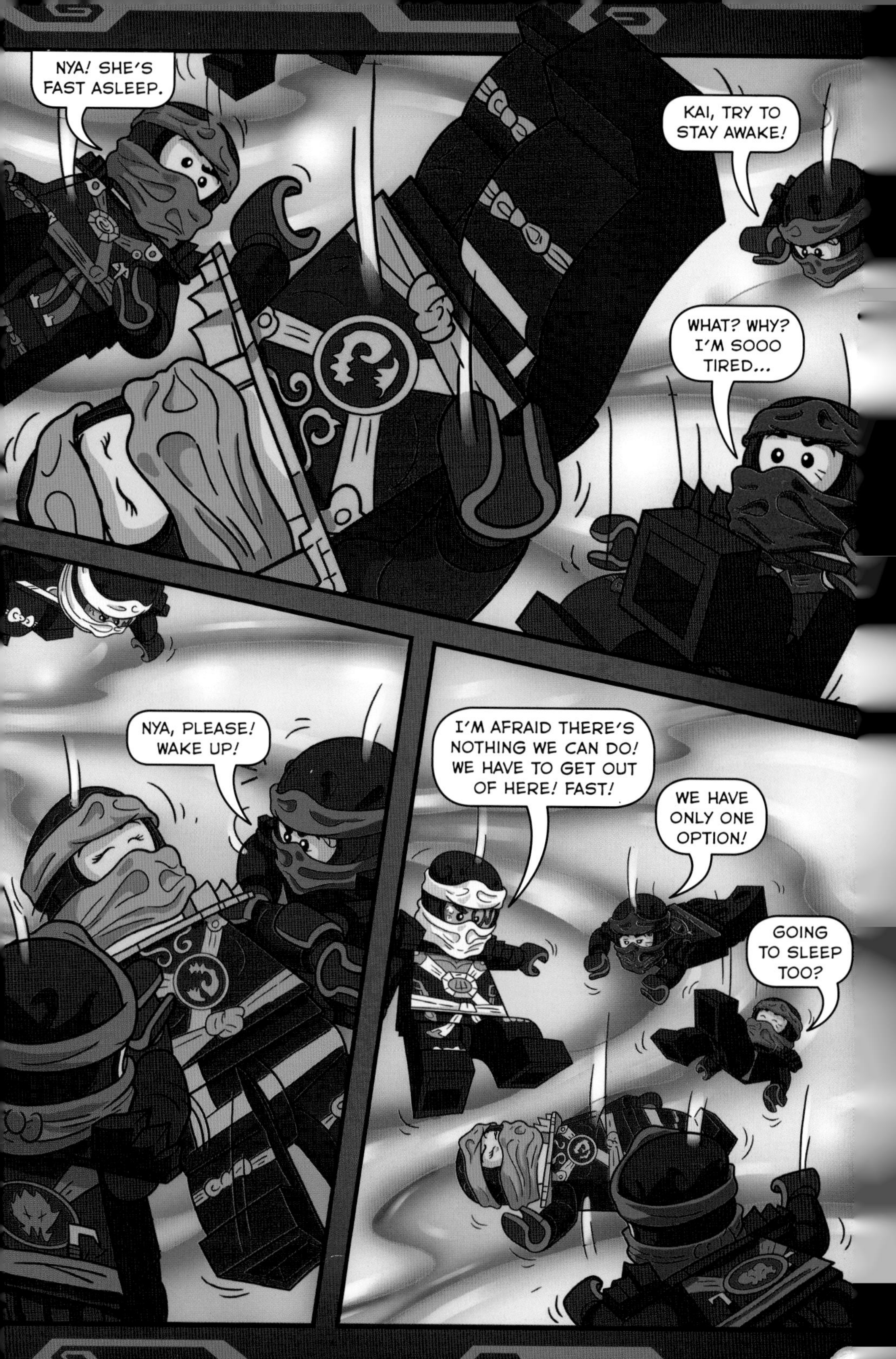
NYA! SHE'S FAST ASLEEP.
KAI, TRY TO STAY AWAKE!
WHAT? WHY? I'M SOOO TIRED...
NYA, PLEASE! WAKE UP!
I'M AFRAID THERE'S NOTHING WE CAN DO! WE HAVE TO GET OUT OF HERE! FAST!
WE HAVE ONLY ONE OPTION!
GOING TO SLEEP TOO?

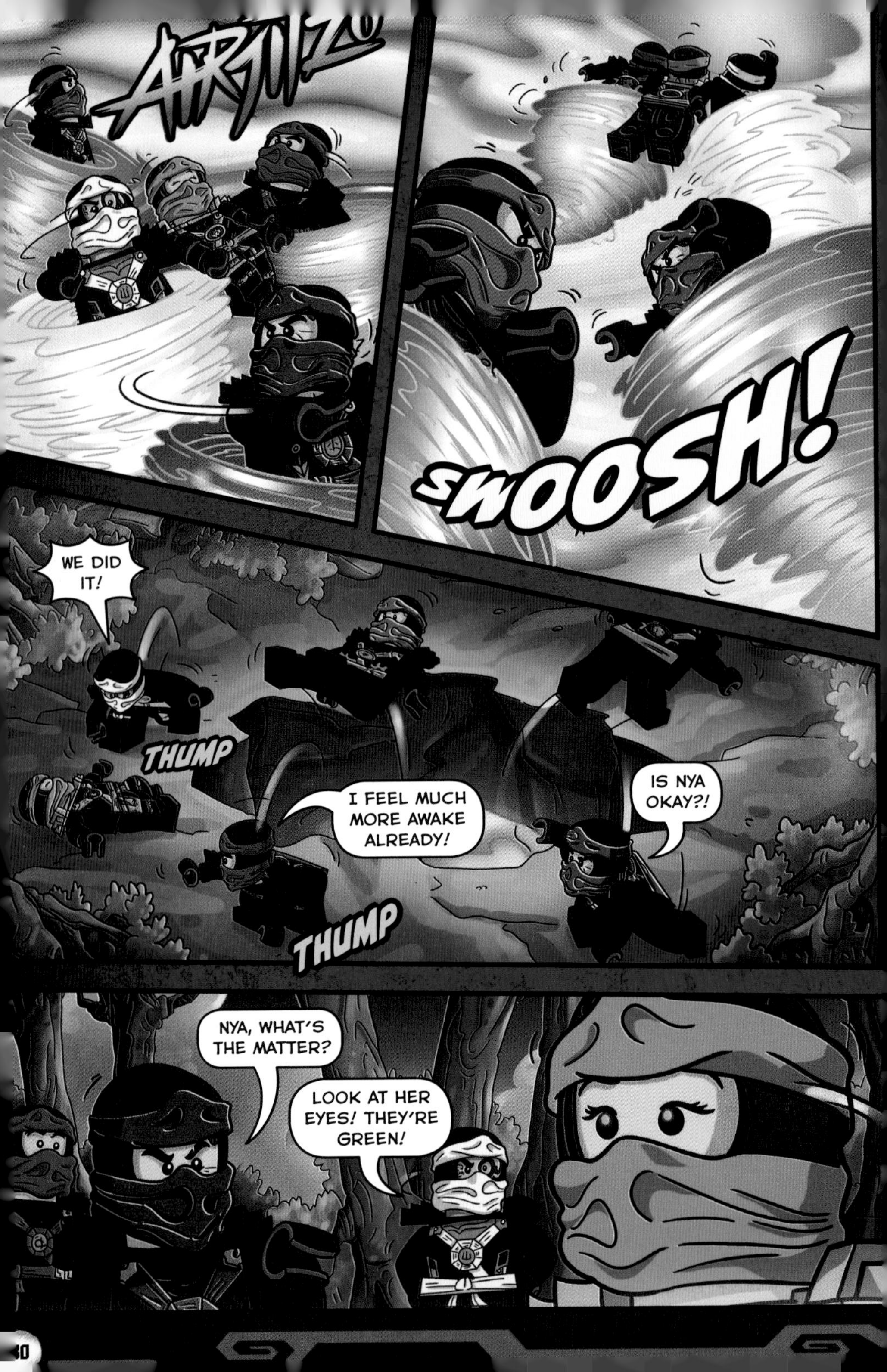
AIRJITZU
SWOOSH!
WE DID IT!
THUMP
I FEEL MUCH MORE AWAKE ALREADY!
IS NYA OKAY?!
THUMP
NYA, WHAT'S THE MATTER?
LOOK AT HER EYES! THEY'RE GREEN!

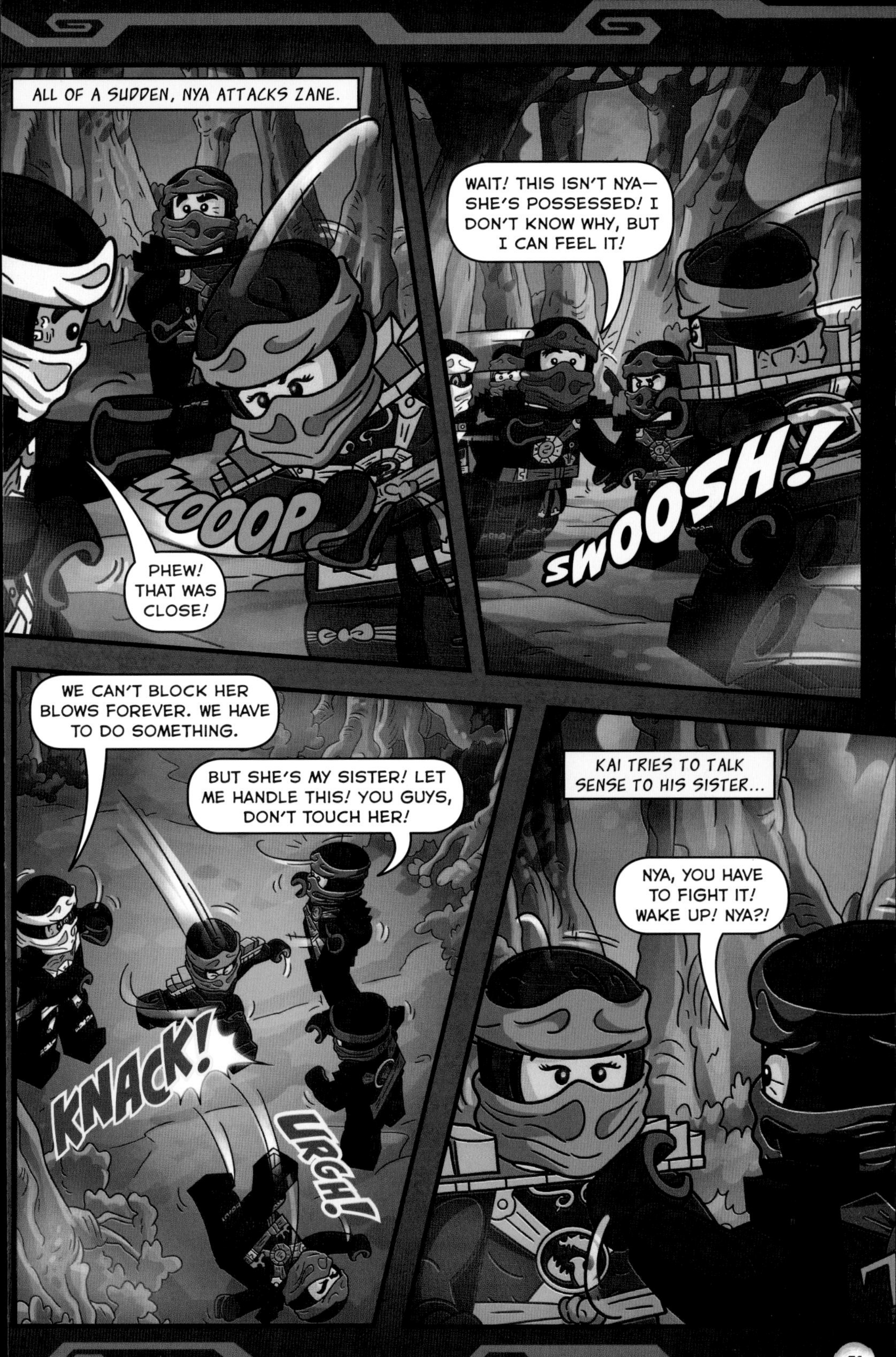
ALL OF A SUDDEN, NYA ATTACKS ZANE.
WOOOP
PHEW! THAT WAS CLOSE!
WAIT! THIS ISN'T NYA—SHE'S POSSESSED! I DON'T KNOW WHY, BUT I CAN FEEL IT!
SWOOSH!
WE CAN'T BLOCK HER BLOWS FOREVER. WE HAVE TO DO SOMETHING.
BUT SHE'S MY SISTER! LET ME HANDLE THIS! YOU GUYS, DON'T TOUCH HER!
KNACK!
URGH!
KAI TRIES TO TALK SENSE TO HIS SISTER...
NYA, YOU HAVE TO FIGHT IT! WAKE UP! NYA?!

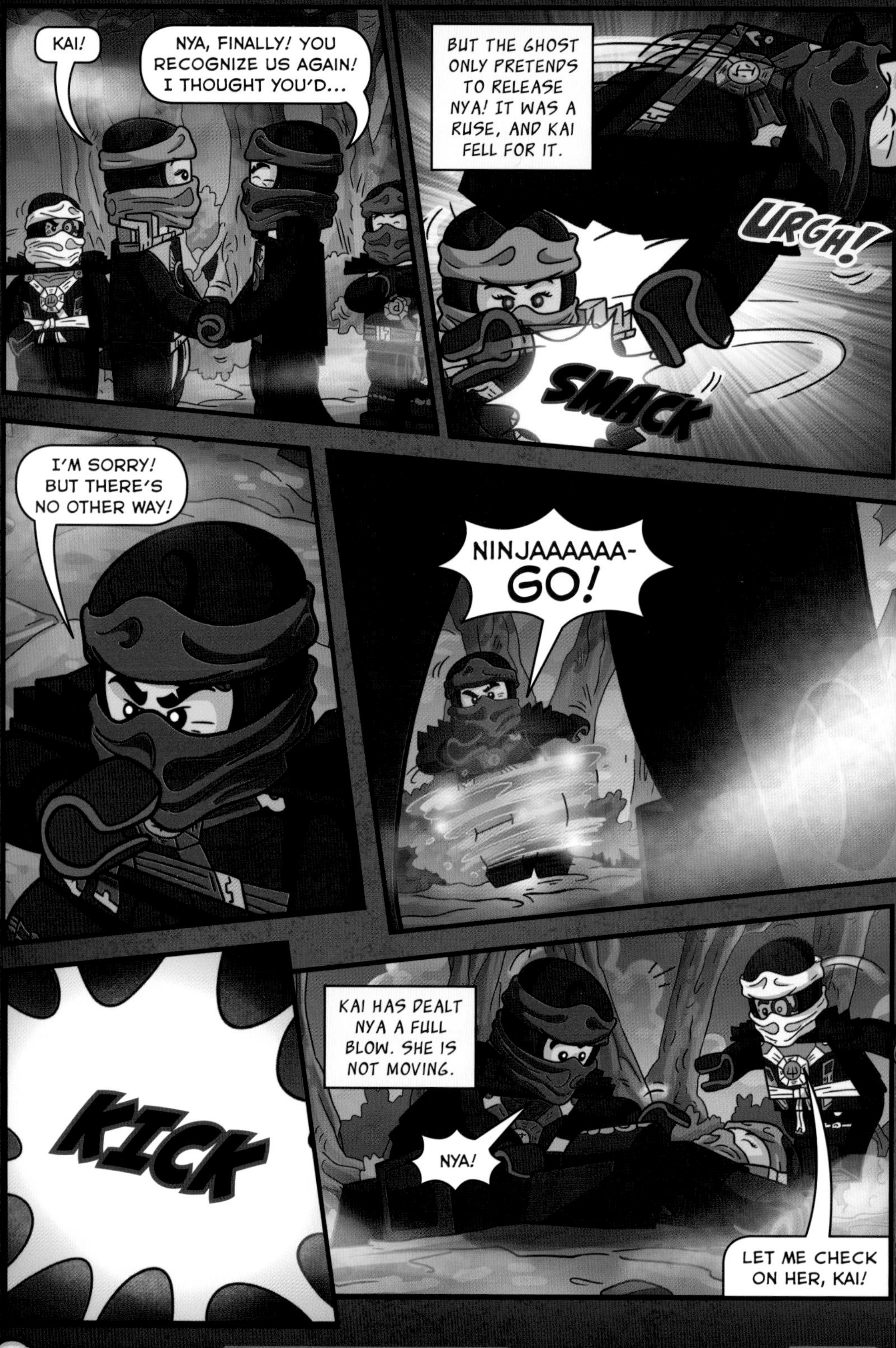
KAI!
NYA, FINALLY! YOU RECOGNIZE US AGAIN! I THOUGHT YOU'D...
BUT THE GHOST ONLY PRETENDS TO RELEASE NYA! IT WAS A RUSE, AND KAI FELL FOR IT.
URGH!
SMACK
I'M SORRY! BUT THERE'S NO OTHER WAY!
NINJAAAAAA-GO!
KICK
KAI HAS DEALT NYA A FULL BLOW. SHE IS NOT MOVING.
NYA!
LET ME CHECK ON HER, KAI!

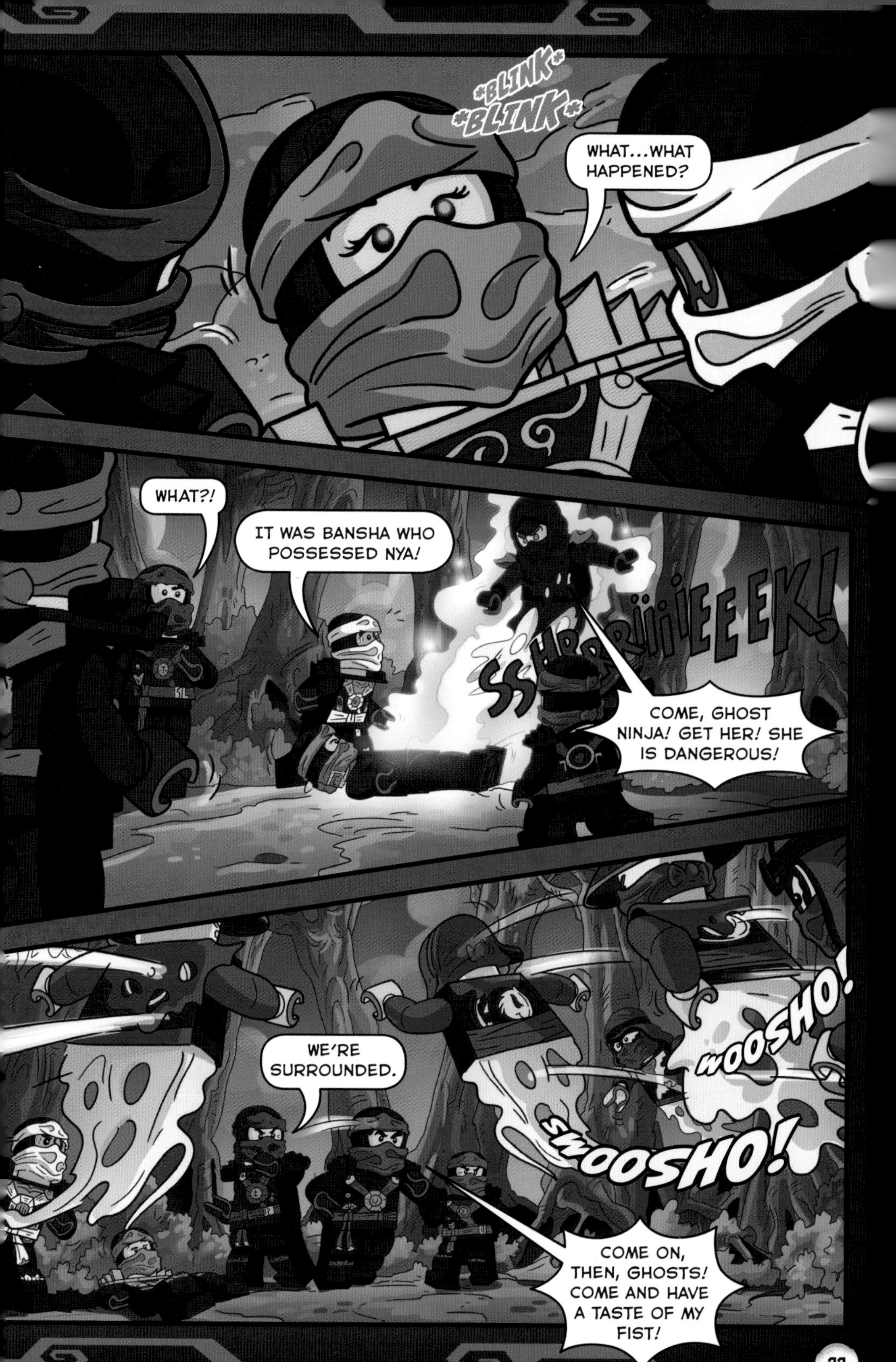
BLINK
BLINK
WHAT...WHAT HAPPENED?
WHAT?!
IT WAS BANSHA WHO POSSESSED NYA!
SSHRRRIIIIEEEK!
COME, GHOST NINJA! GET HER! SHE IS DANGEROUS!
WE'RE SURROUNDED.
WOOSHO!
SWOOSHO!
COME ON, THEN, GHOSTS! COME AND HAVE A TASTE OF MY FIST!

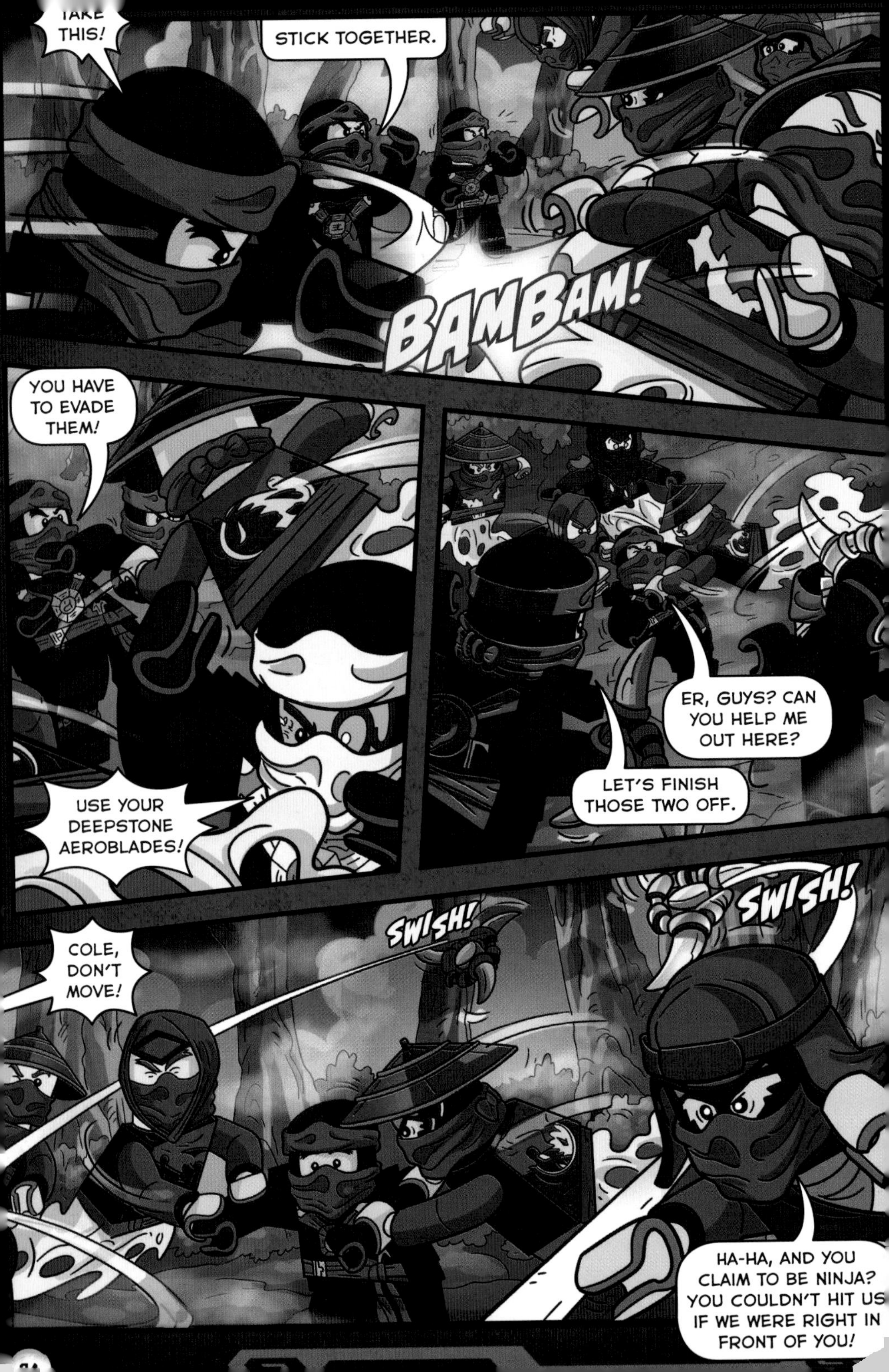
TAKE THIS!
STICK TOGETHER.
BAMBAM!
YOU HAVE TO EVADE THEM!
USE YOUR DEEPSTONE AEROBLADES!
ER, GUYS? CAN YOU HELP ME OUT HERE?
LET'S FINISH THOSE TWO OFF.
SWISH!
SWISH!
COLE, DON'T MOVE!
HA-HA, AND YOU CLAIM TO BE NINJA? YOU COULDN'T HIT US IF WE WERE RIGHT IN FRONT OF YOU!

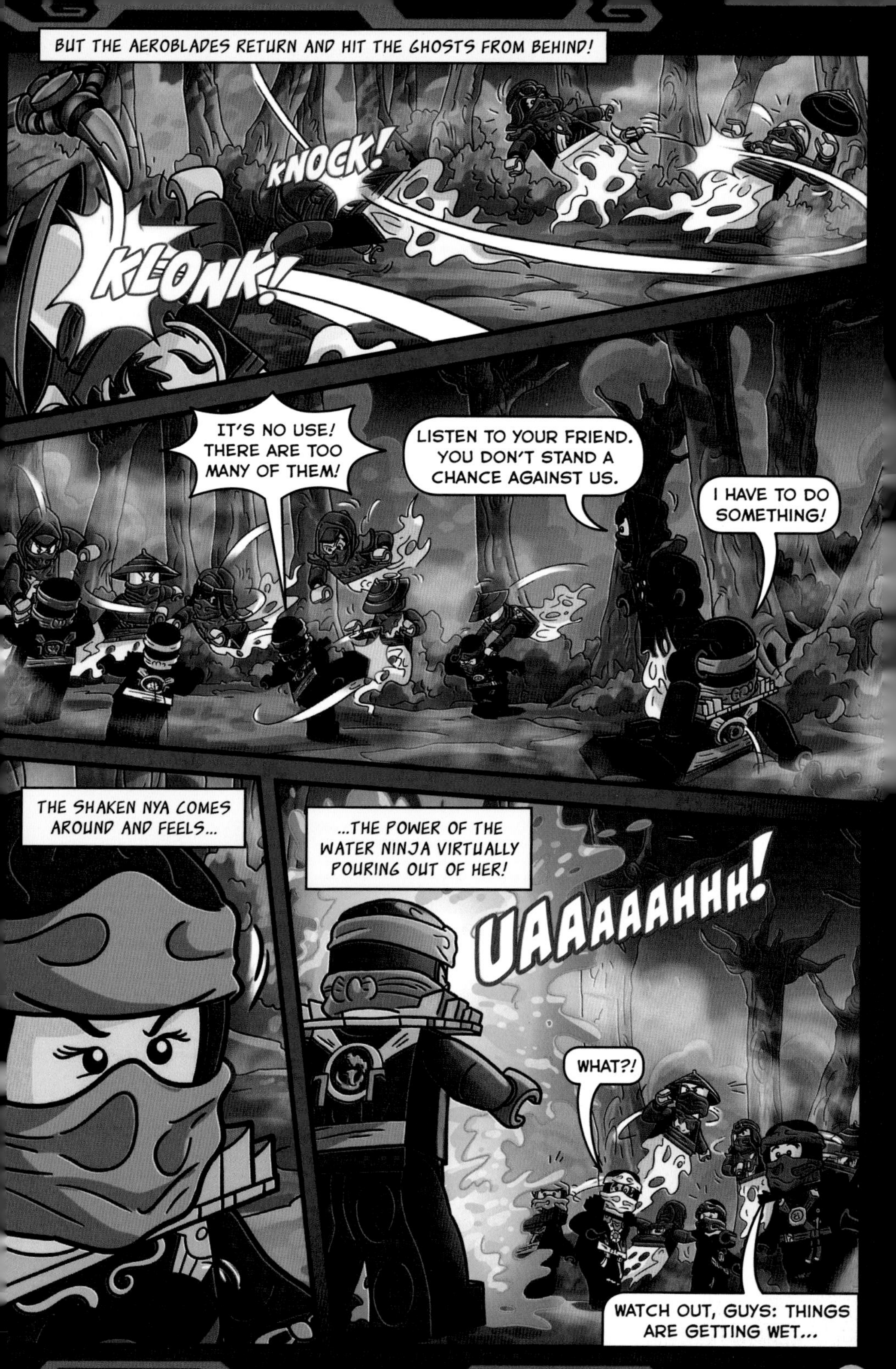
BUT THE AEROBLADES RETURN AND HIT THE GHOSTS FROM BEHIND!
KNOCK!
KLONK!
IT'S NO USE! THERE ARE TOO MANY OF THEM!
LISTEN TO YOUR FRIEND. YOU DON'T STAND A CHANCE AGAINST US.
I HAVE TO DO SOMETHING!
THE SHAKEN NYA COMES AROUND AND FEELS...
...THE POWER OF THE WATER NINJA VIRTUALLY POURING OUT OF HER!
UAAAAAHHH!
WHAT?!
WATCH OUT, GUYS: THINGS ARE GETTING WET...

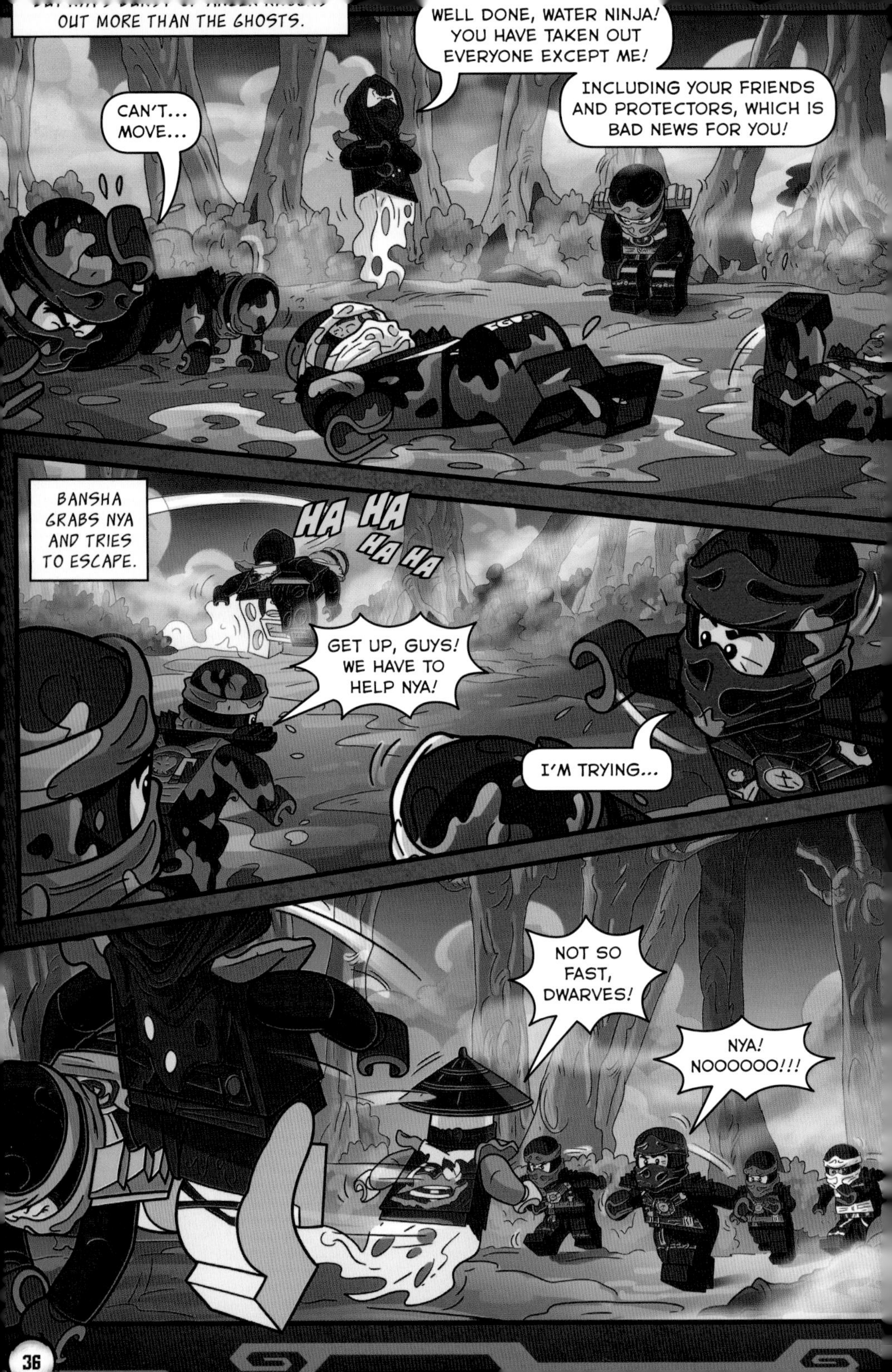
OUT MORE THAN THE GHOSTS.
WELL DONE, WATER NINJA! YOU HAVE TAKEN OUT EVERYONE EXCEPT ME!
INCLUDING YOUR FRIENDS AND PROTECTORS, WHICH IS BAD NEWS FOR YOU!
CAN'T... MOVE...
BANSHA GRABS NYA AND TRIES TO ESCAPE.
HA HA HA HA
GET UP, GUYS! WE HAVE TO HELP NYA!
I'M TRYING...
NOT SO FAST, DWARVES!
NYA! NOOOOOO!!!

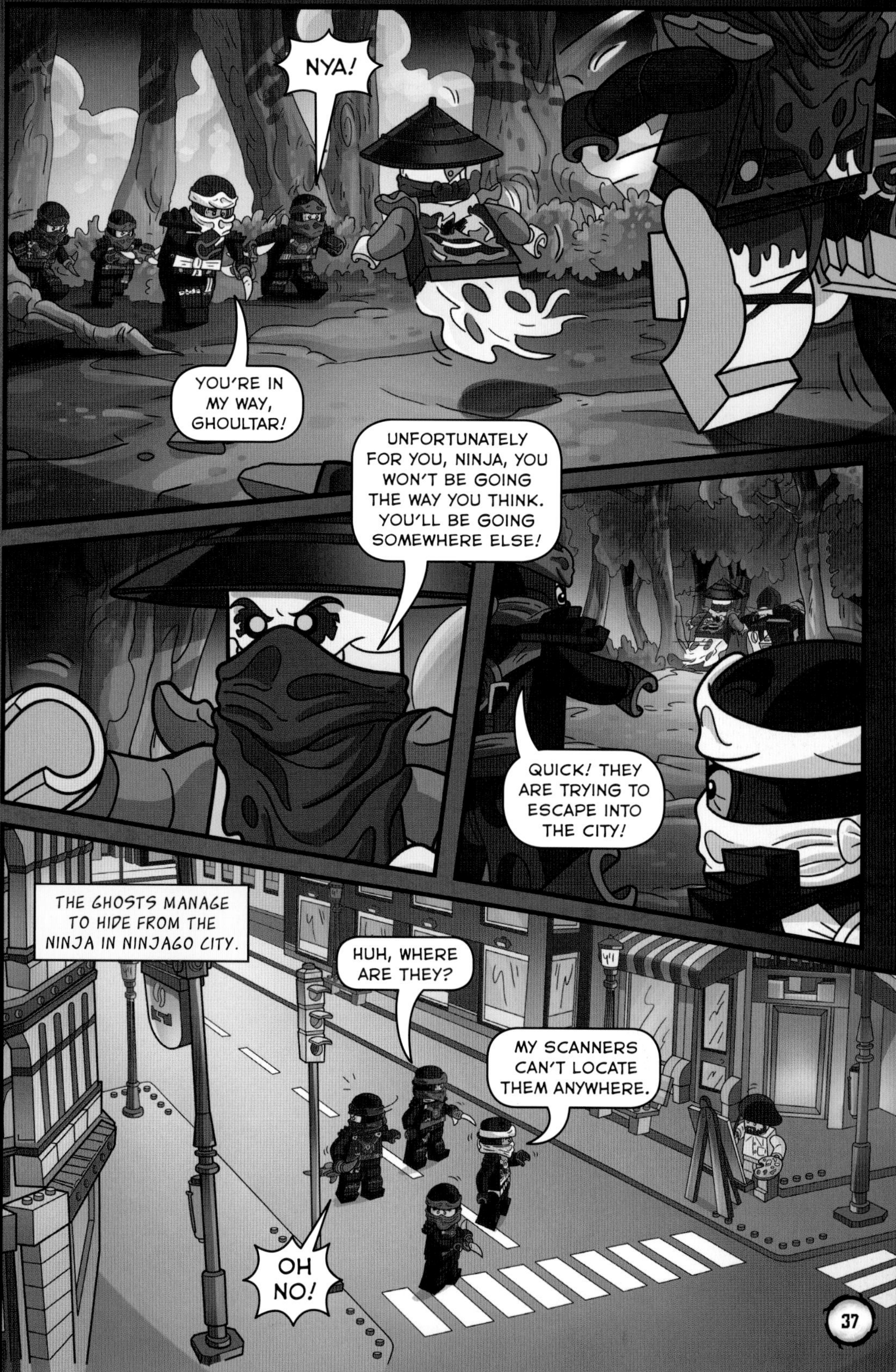
NYA!
YOU'RE IN MY WAY, GHOULTAR!
UNFORTUNATELY FOR YOU, NINJA, YOU WON'T BE GOING THE WAY YOU THINK. YOU'LL BE GOING SOMEWHERE ELSE!
QUICK! THEY ARE TRYING TO ESCAPE INTO THE CITY!
THE GHOSTS MANAGE TO HIDE FROM THE NINJA IN NINJAGO CITY.
HUH, WHERE ARE THEY?
MY SCANNERS CAN'T LOCATE THEM ANYWHERE.
OH NO!

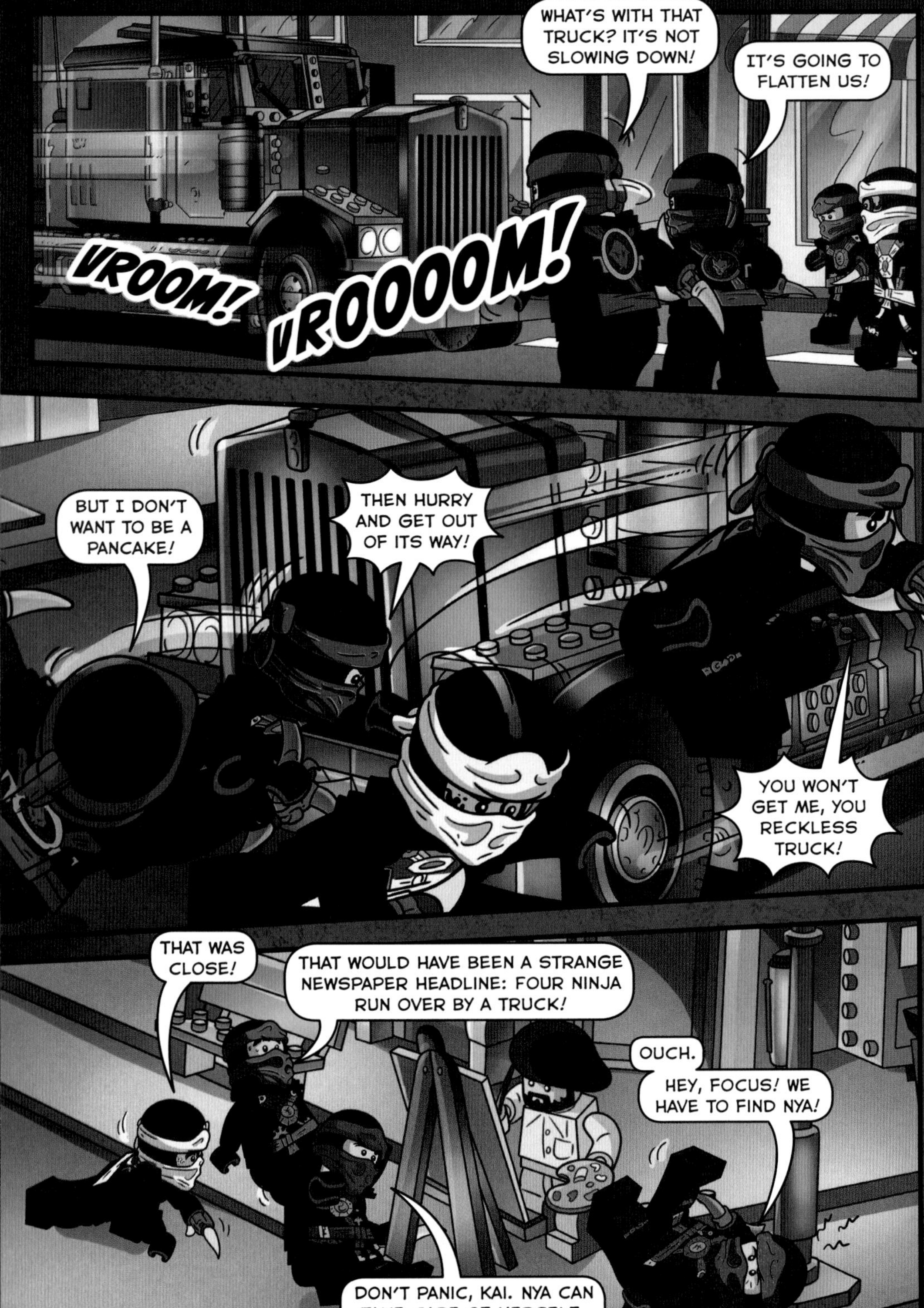
WHAT'S WITH THAT TRUCK? IT'S NOT SLOWING DOWN!
IT'S GOING TO FLATTEN US!
VROOM!
VROOOOM!
BUT I DON'T WANT TO BE A PANCAKE!
THEN HURRY AND GET OUT OF ITS WAY!
YOU WON'T GET ME, YOU RECKLESS TRUCK!
THAT WAS CLOSE!
THAT WOULD HAVE BEEN A STRANGE NEWSPAPER HEADLINE: FOUR NINJA RUN OVER BY A TRUCK!
OUCH.
HEY, FOCUS! WE HAVE TO FIND NYA!
DON'T PANIC, KAI. NYA CAN TAKE CARE OF HERSELF.

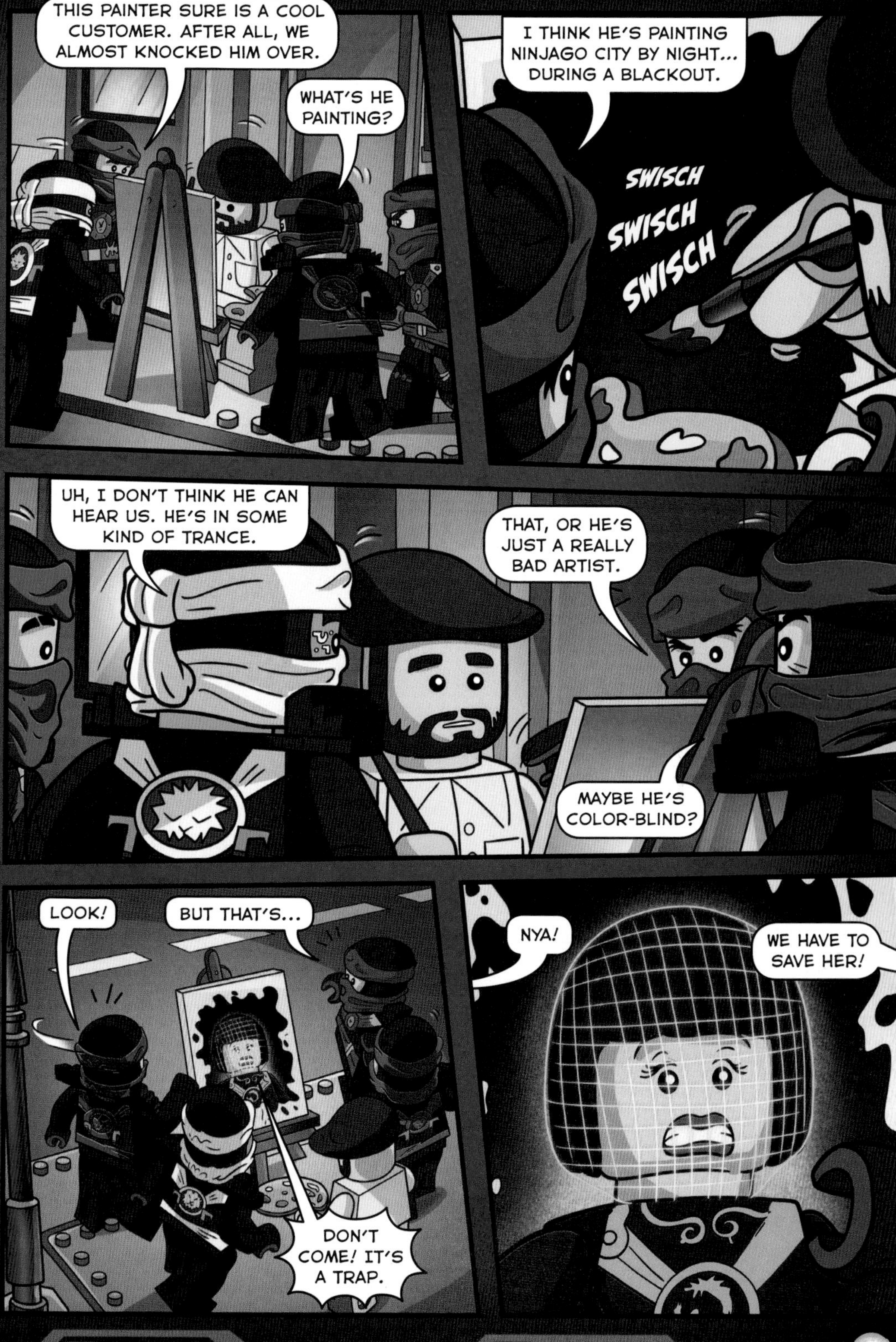
THIS PAINTER SURE IS A COOL CUSTOMER. AFTER ALL, WE ALMOST KNOCKED HIM OVER.
WHAT'S HE PAINTING?
I THINK HE'S PAINTING NINJAGO CITY BY NIGHT... DURING A BLACKOUT.
SWISCH
SWISCH
SWISCH
UH, I DON'T THINK HE CAN HEAR US. HE'S IN SOME KIND OF TRANCE.
THAT, OR HE'S JUST A REALLY BAD ARTIST.
MAYBE HE'S COLOR-BLIND?
LOOK!
BUT THAT'S...
DON'T COME! IT'S A TRAP.
NYA!
WE HAVE TO SAVE HER!

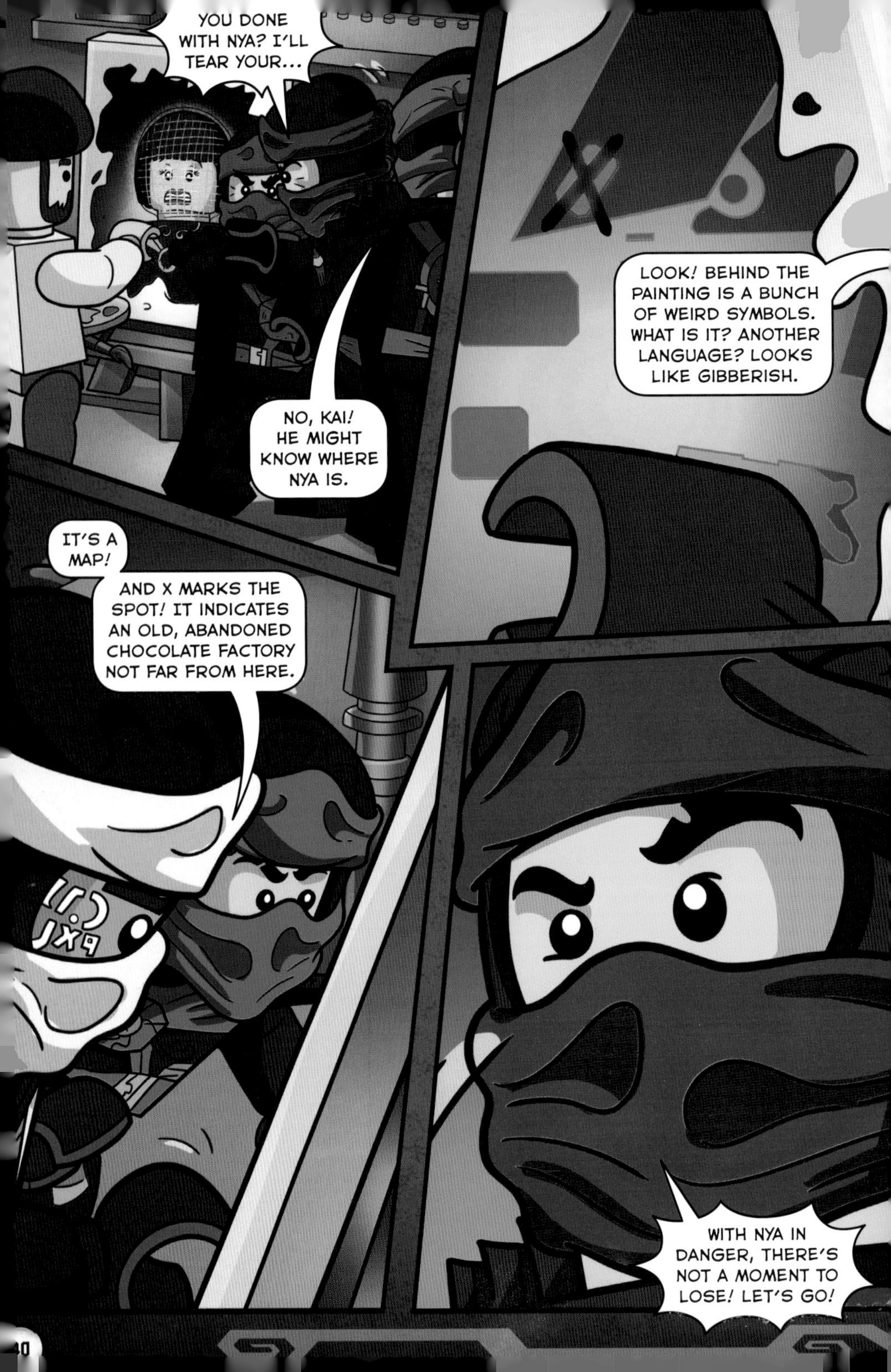

YOU DONE WITH NYA? I'LL TEAR YOUR...
NO, KAI! HE MIGHT KNOW WHERE NYA IS.
LOOK! BEHIND THE PAINTING IS A BUNCH OF WEIRD SYMBOLS. WHAT IS IT? ANOTHER LANGUAGE? LOOKS LIKE GIBBERISH.
IT'S A MAP!
AND X MARKS THE SPOT! IT INDICATES AN OLD, ABANDONED CHOCOLATE FACTORY NOT FAR FROM HERE.
WITH NYA IN DANGER, THERE'S NOT A MOMENT TO LOSE! LET'S GO!

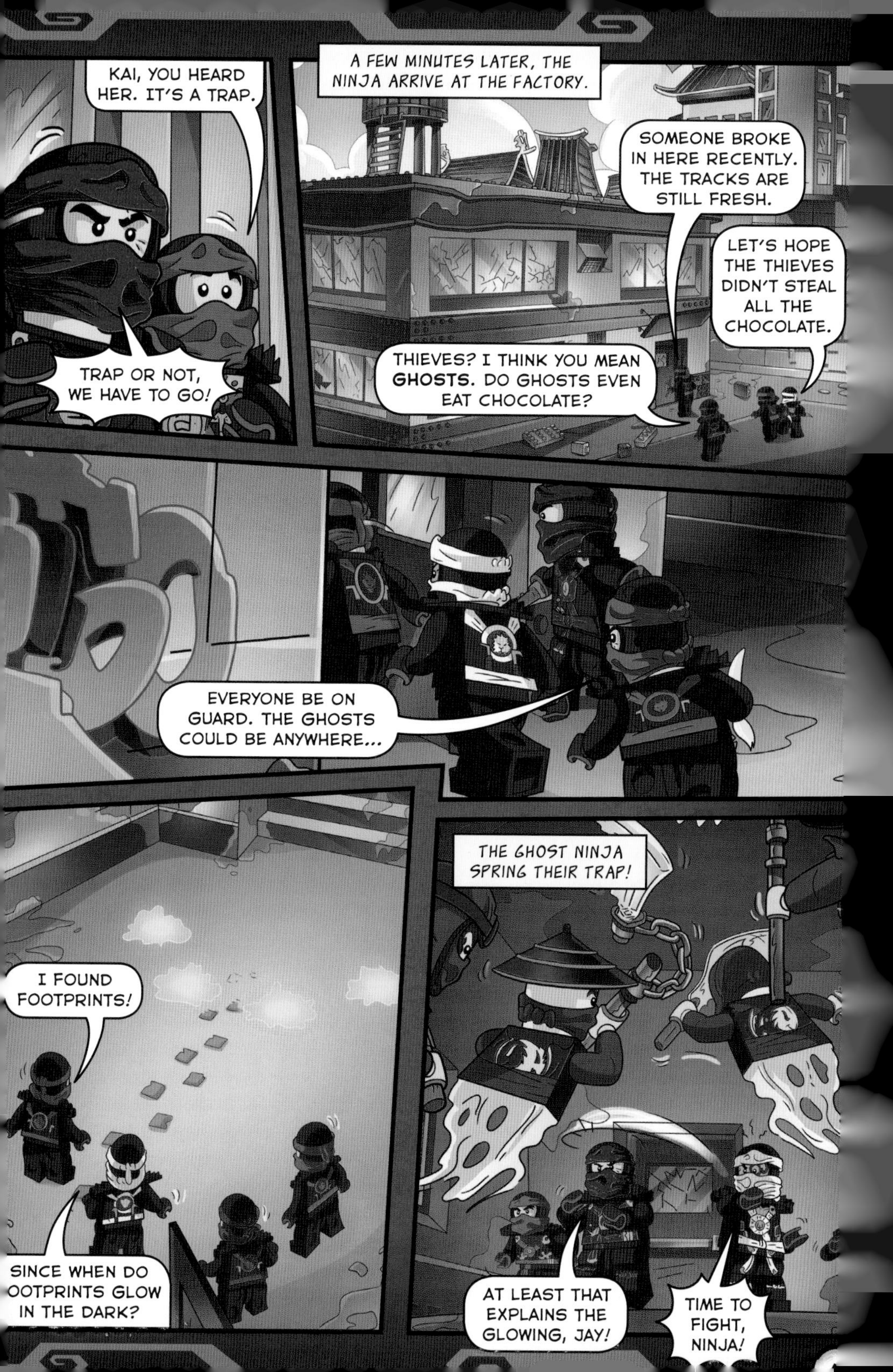
KAI, YOU HEARD HER. IT'S A TRAP.
TRAP OR NOT, WE HAVE TO GO!
A FEW MINUTES LATER, THE NINJA ARRIVE AT THE FACTORY.
SOMEONE BROKE IN HERE RECENTLY. THE TRACKS ARE STILL FRESH.
LET'S HOPE THE THIEVES DIDN'T STEAL ALL THE CHOCOLATE.
THIEVES? I THINK YOU MEAN GHOSTS. DO GHOSTS EVEN EAT CHOCOLATE?
EVERYONE BE ON GUARD. THE GHOSTS COULD BE ANYWHERE...
I FOUND FOOTPRINTS!
SINCE WHEN DO OOTPRINTS GLOW IN THE DARK?
THE GHOST NINJA SPRING THEIR TRAP!
AT LEAST THAT EXPLAINS THE GLOWING, JAY!
TIME TO FIGHT, NINJA!

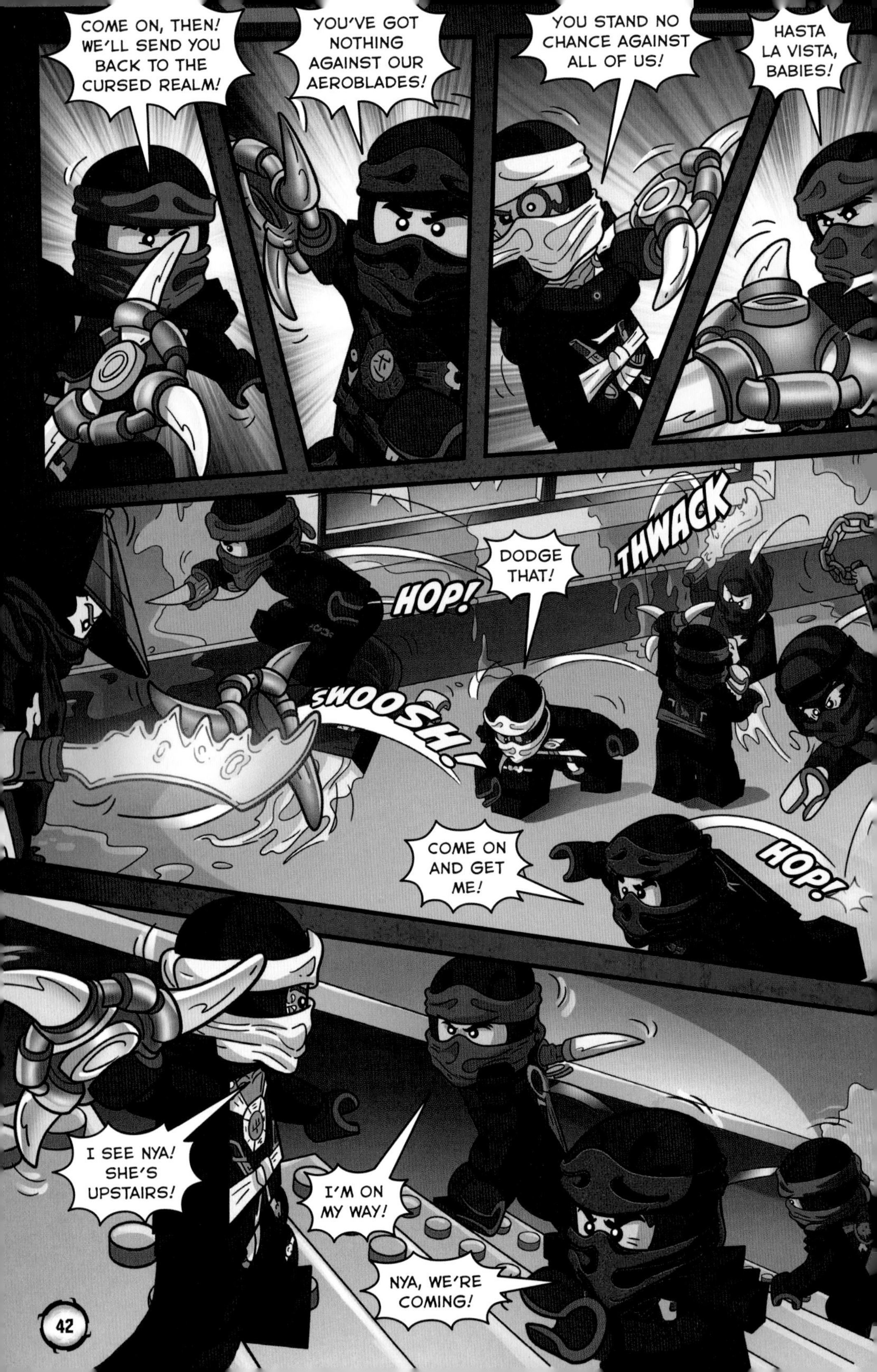

COME ON, THEN! WE'LL SEND YOU BACK TO THE CURSED REALM!
YOU'VE GOT NOTHING AGAINST OUR AEROBLADES!
YOU STAND NO CHANCE AGAINST ALL OF US!
HASTA LA VISTA, BABIES!
THWACK
HOP!
DODGE THAT!
SWOOSH!
COME ON AND GET ME!
HOP!
I SEE NYA! SHE'S UPSTAIRS!
I'M ON MY WAY!
NYA, WE'RE COMING!

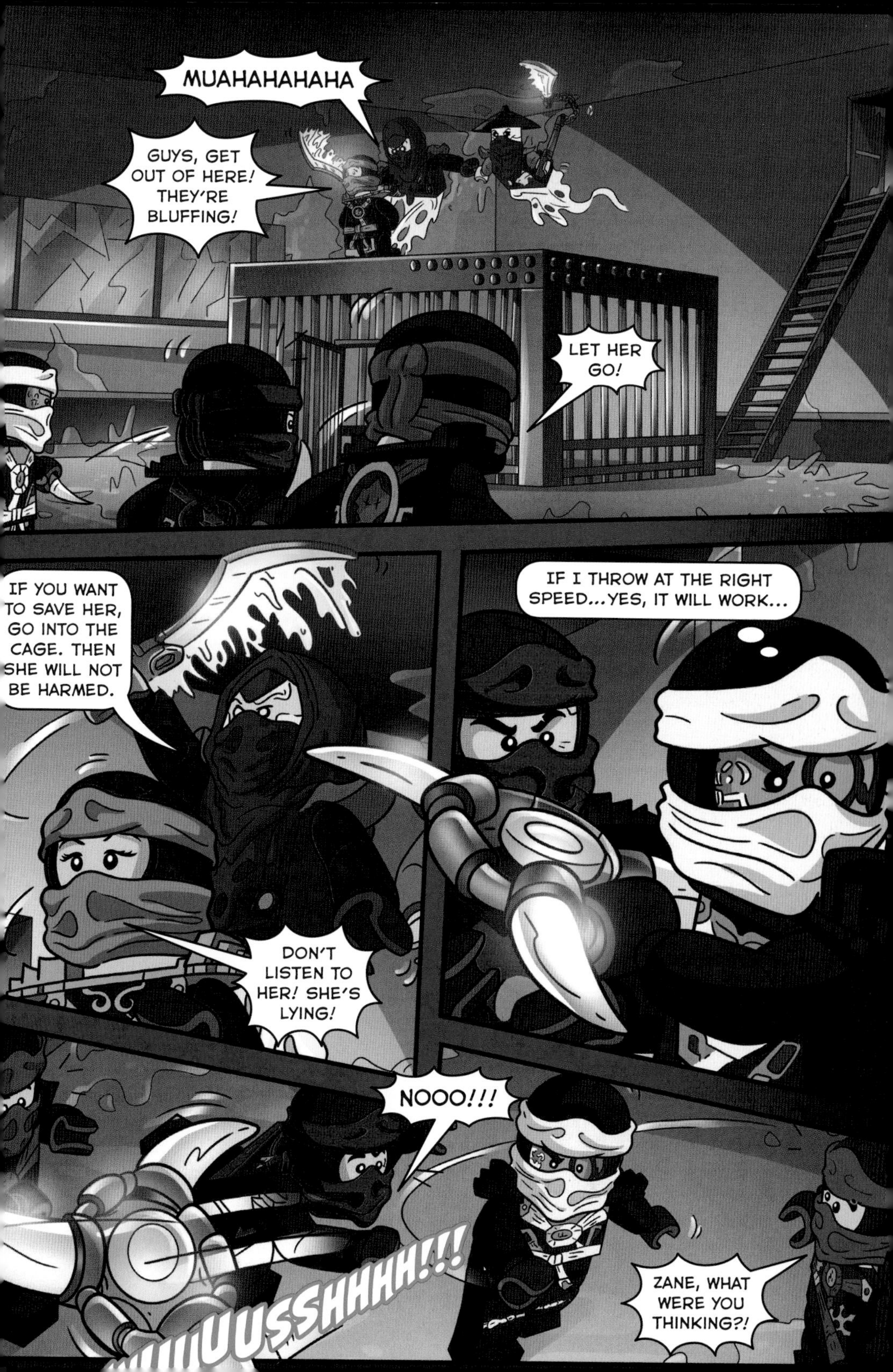
MUAHAHAHAHA
GUYS, GET OUT OF HERE! THEY'RE BLUFFING!
LET HER GO!
IF YOU WANT TO SAVE HER, GO INTO THE CAGE. THEN SHE WILL NOT BE HARMED.
DON'T LISTEN TO HER! SHE'S LYING!
IF I THROW AT THE RIGHT SPEED...YES, IT WILL WORK...
NOOO!!!
UUSSHHHH!!!
ZANE, WHAT WERE YOU THINKING?!

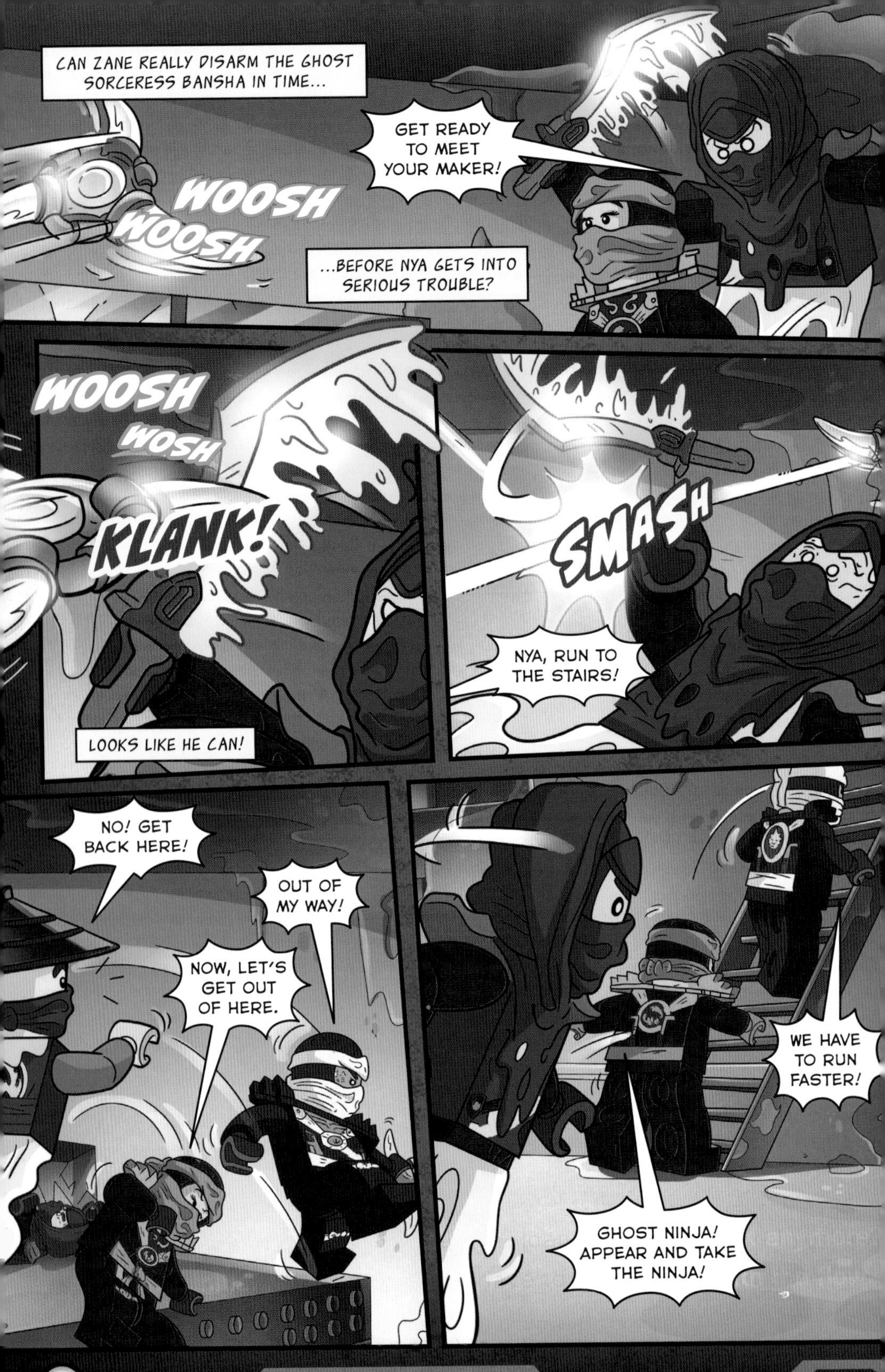
CAN ZANE REALLY DISARM THE GHOST SORCERESS BANSHA IN TIME...
GET READY TO MEET YOUR MAKER!
WOOSH
WOOSH
...BEFORE NYA GETS INTO SERIOUS TROUBLE?
WOOSH
WOSH
KLANK!
LOOKS LIKE HE CAN!
SMASH
NYA, RUN TO THE STAIRS!
NO! GET BACK HERE!
OUT OF MY WAY!
NOW, LET'S GET OUT OF HERE.
WE HAVE TO RUN FASTER!
GHOST NINJA! APPEAR AND TAKE THE NINJA!

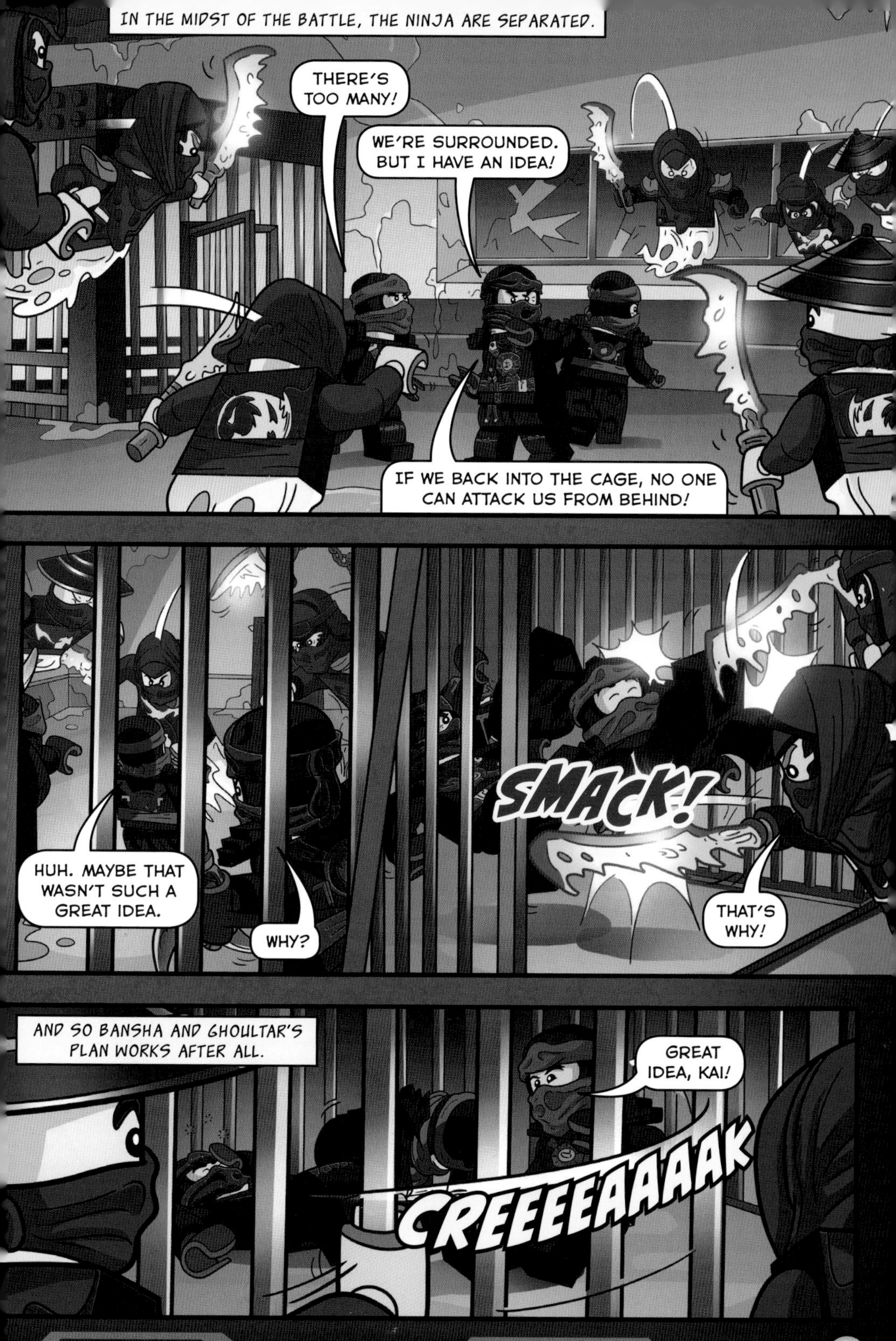

IN THE MIDST OF THE BATTLE, THE NINJA ARE SEPARATED.
THERE'S TOO MANY!
WE'RE SURROUNDED. BUT I HAVE AN IDEA!
IF WE BACK INTO THE CAGE, NO ONE CAN ATTACK US FROM BEHIND!
SMACK!
HUH. MAYBE THAT WASN'T SUCH A GREAT IDEA.
WHY?
THAT'S WHY!
AND SO BANSHA AND GHOULTAR'S PLAN WORKS AFTER ALL.
GREAT IDEA, KAI!
CREEEEAAAAK

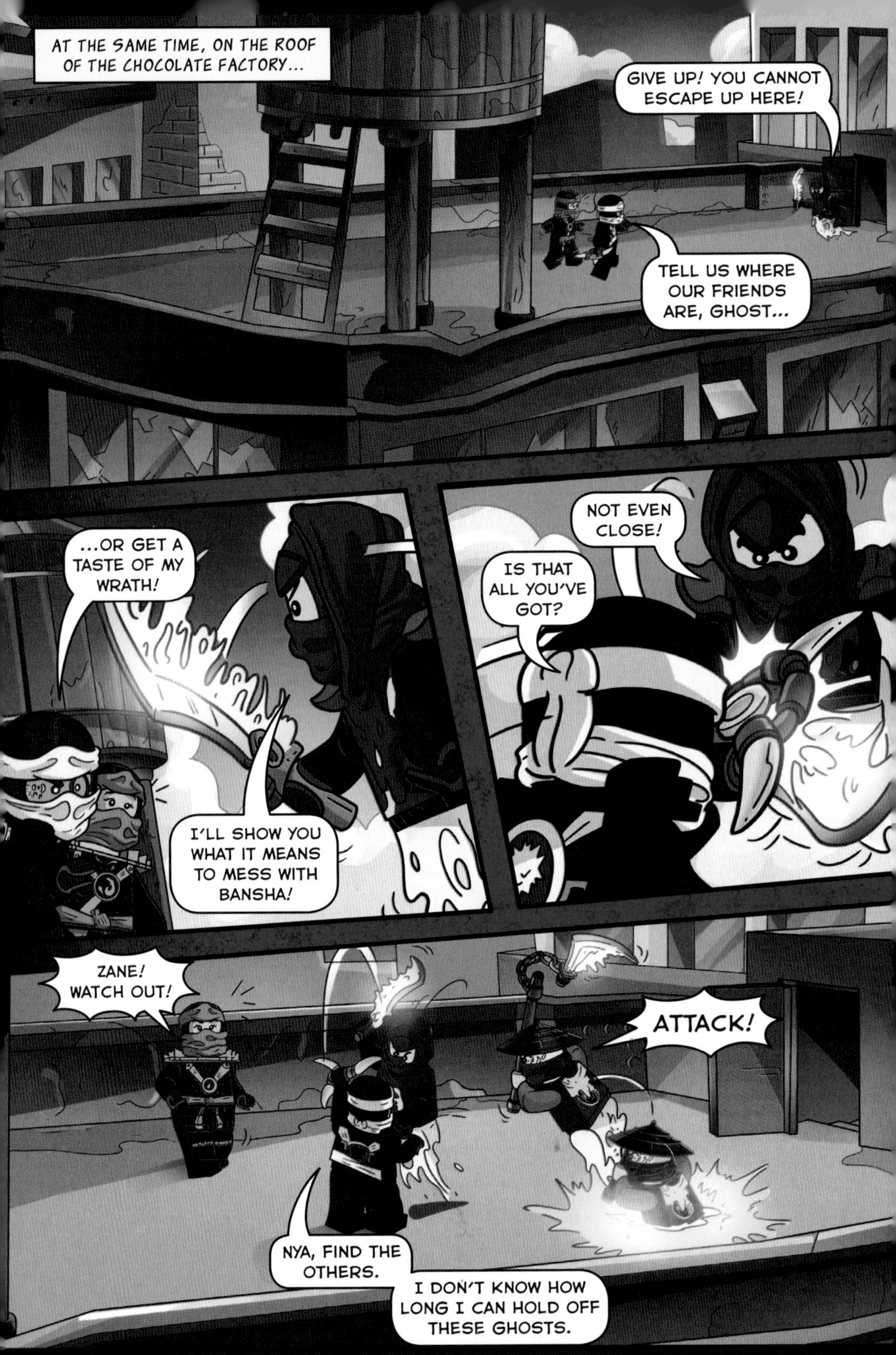
AT THE SAME TIME, ON THE ROOF OF THE CHOCOLATE FACTORY...
GIVE UP! YOU CANNOT ESCAPE UP HERE!
TELL US WHERE OUR FRIENDS ARE, GHOST...
...OR GET A TASTE OF MY WRATH!
I'LL SHOW YOU WHAT IT MEANS TO MESS WITH BANSHA!
NOT EVEN CLOSE!
IS THAT ALL YOU'VE GOT?
ZANE! WATCH OUT!
ATTACK!
NYA, FIND THE OTHERS.
I DON'T KNOW HOW LONG I CAN HOLD OFF THESE GHOSTS.

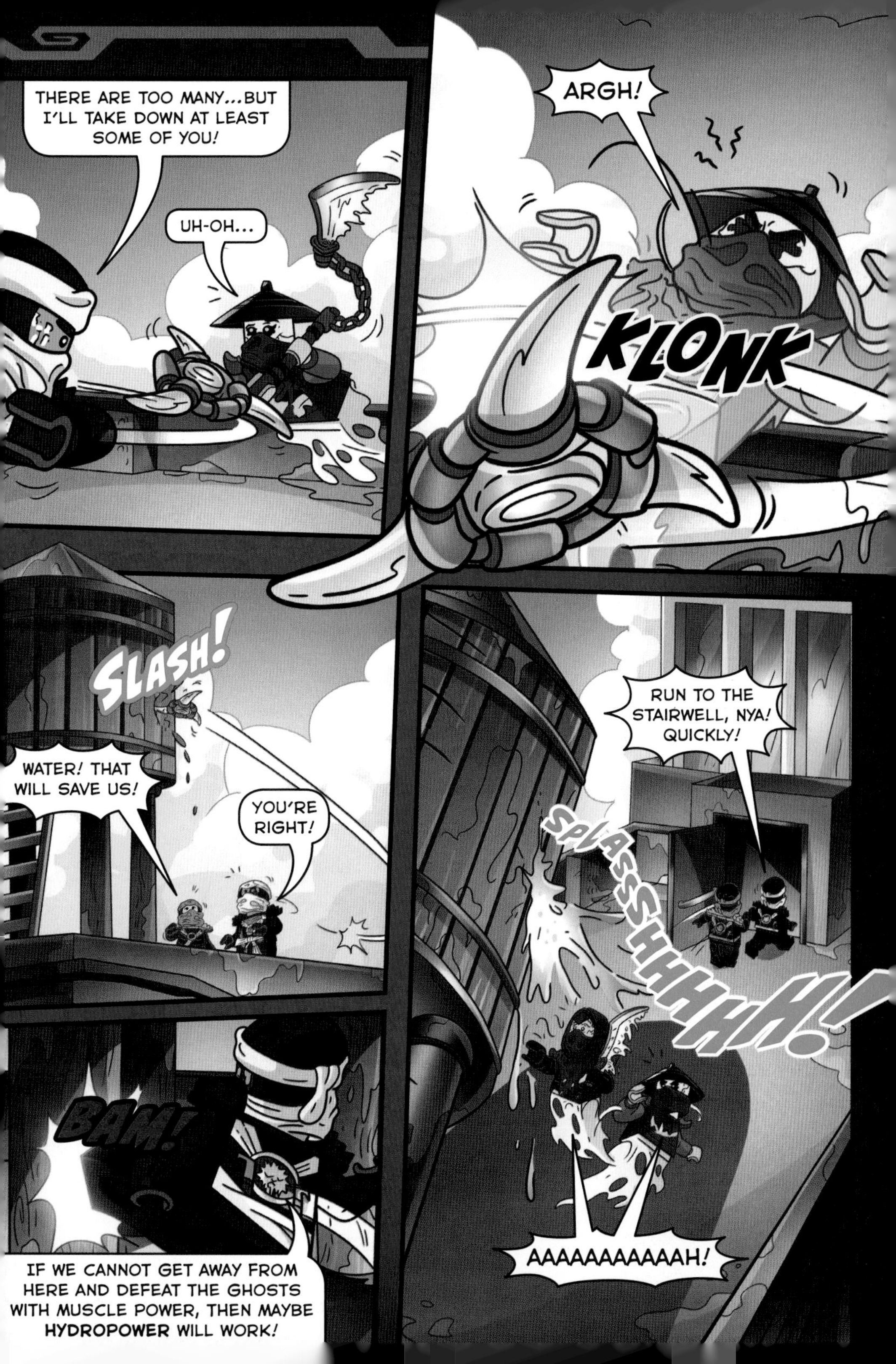
THERE ARE TOO MANY...BUT I'LL TAKE DOWN AT LEAST SOME OF YOU!
UH-OH...
ARGH!
KLONK
SLASH!
WATER! THAT WILL SAVE US!
YOU'RE RIGHT!
IF WE CANNOT GET AWAY FROM HERE AND DEFEAT THE GHOSTS WITH MUSCLE POWER, THEN MAYBE HYDROPOWER WILL WORK!
BAM!
RUN TO THE STAIRWELL, NYA! QUICKLY!
SPLASSSHHHHHH!!
AAAAAAAAAAAH!

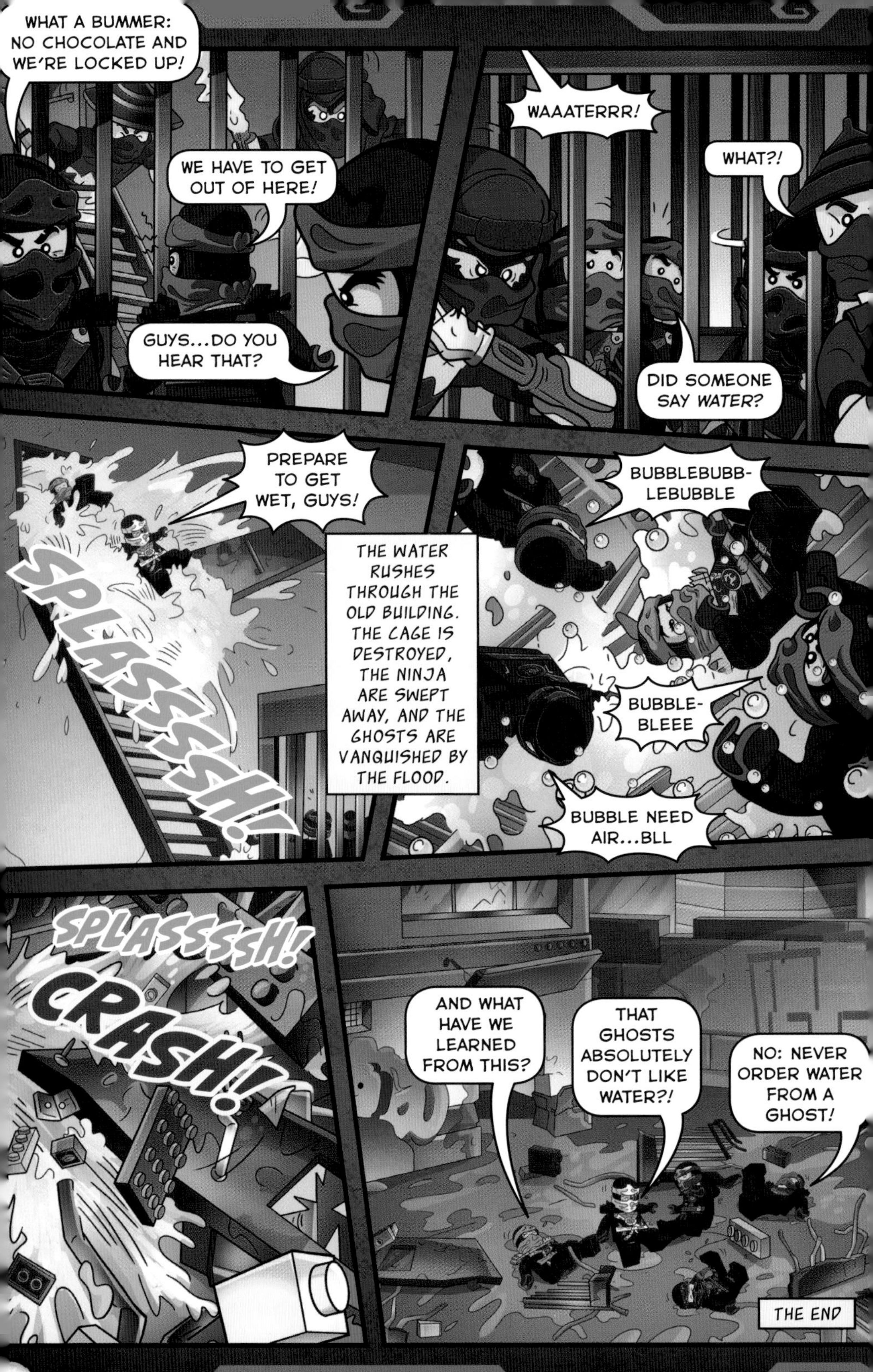
WHAT A BUMMER: NO CHOCOLATE AND WE'RE LOCKED UP!
WE HAVE TO GET OUT OF HERE!
GUYS...DO YOU HEAR THAT?
WAAATERRR!
WHAT?!
DID SOMEONE SAY WATER?
PREPARE TO GET WET, GUYS!
SPLASSSSH!
THE WATER RUSHES THROUGH THE OLD BUILDING. THE CAGE IS DESTROYED, THE NINJA ARE SWEPT AWAY, AND THE GHOSTS ARE VANQUISHED BY THE FLOOD.
BUBBLEBUBB-LEBUBBLE
BUBBLE-BLEEE
BUBBLE NEED AIR...BLL
SPLASSSSH!
CRASH!
AND WHAT HAVE WE LEARNED FROM THIS?
THAT GHOSTS ABSOLUTELY DON'T LIKE WATER?!
NO: NEVER ORDER WATER FROM A GHOST!
THE END

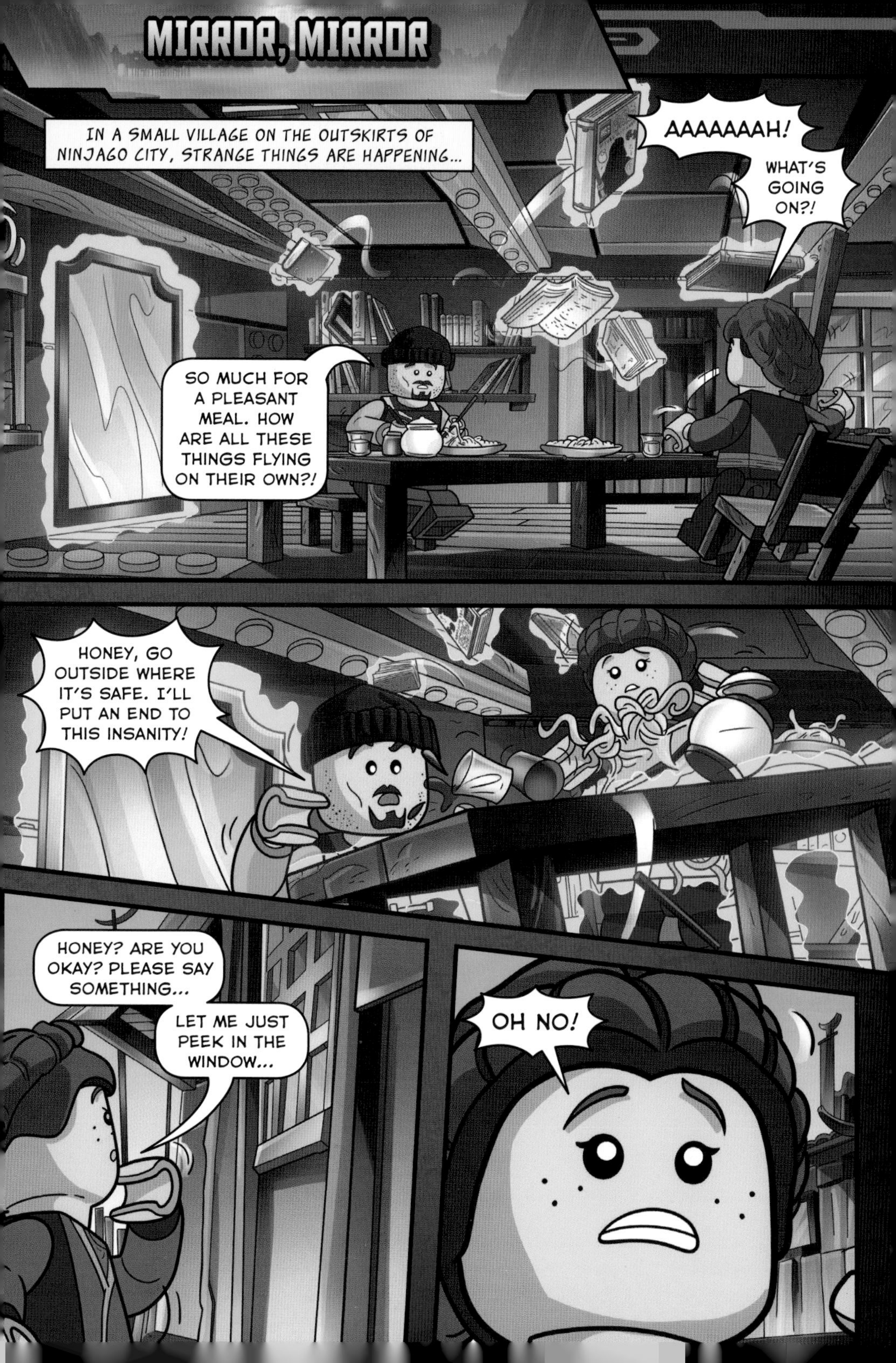
MIRROR, MIRROR
IN A SMALL VILLAGE ON THE OUTSKIRTS OF NINJAGO CITY, STRANGE THINGS ARE HAPPENING...
AAAAAAAH!
WHAT'S GOING ON?!
SO MUCH FOR A PLEASANT MEAL. HOW ARE ALL THESE THINGS FLYING ON THEIR OWN?!
HONEY, GO OUTSIDE WHERE IT'S SAFE. I'LL PUT AN END TO THIS INSANITY!
HONEY? ARE YOU OKAY? PLEASE SAY SOMETHING...
LET ME JUST PEEK IN THE WINDOW...
OH NO!

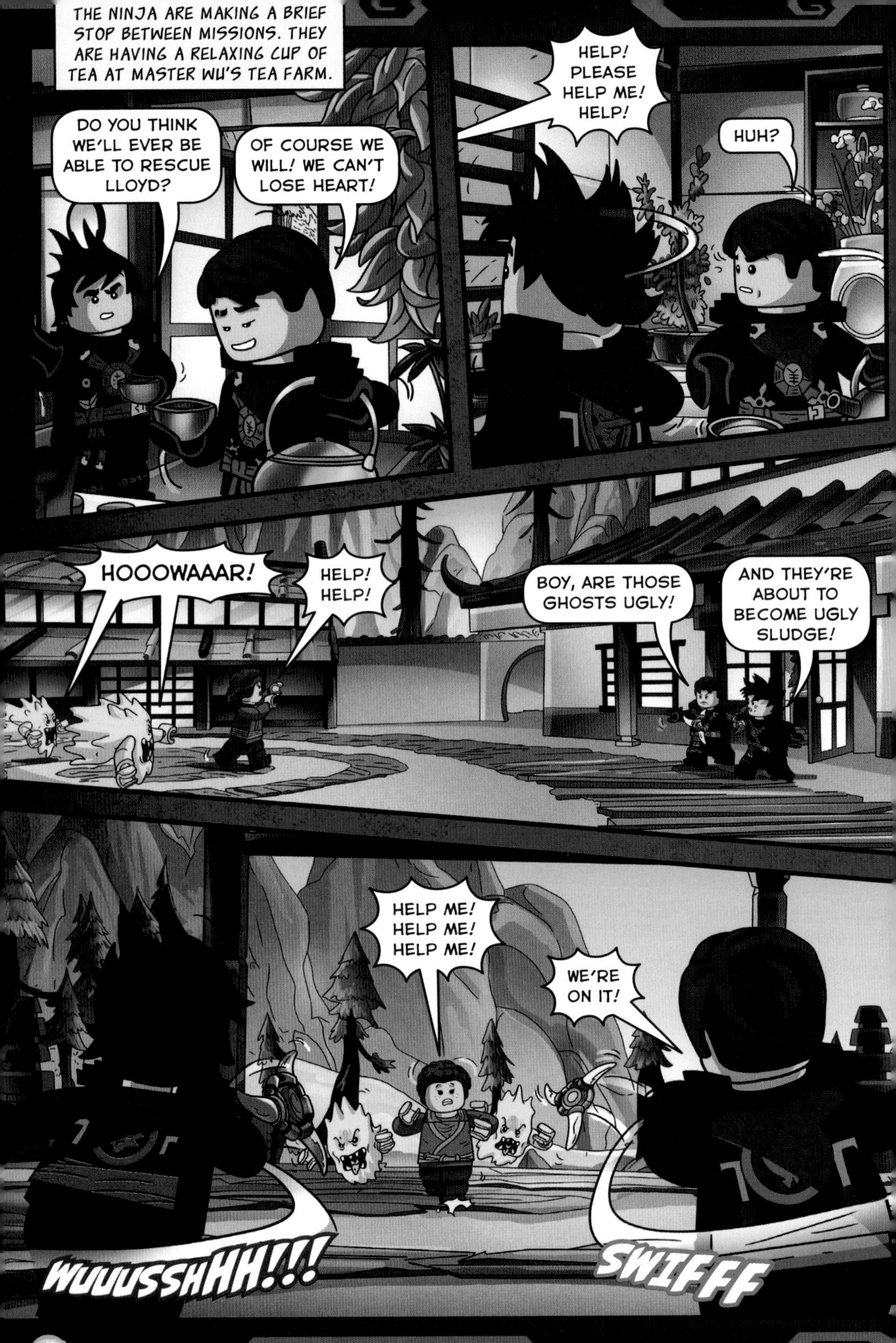
THE NINJA ARE MAKING A BRIEF STOP BETWEEN MISSIONS. THEY ARE HAVING A RELAXING CUP OF TEA AT MASTER WU'S TEA FARM.
DO YOU THINK WE'LL EVER BE ABLE TO RESCUE LLOYD?
OF COURSE WE WILL! WE CAN'T LOSE HEART!
HELP! PLEASE HELP ME! HELP!
HUH?
HOOOWAAAR!
HELP! HELP!
BOY, ARE THOSE GHOSTS UGLY!
AND THEY'RE ABOUT TO BECOME UGLY SLUDGE!
HELP ME! HELP ME! HELP ME!
WE'RE ON IT!
WUUUSSHHH!!!
SWIFFF

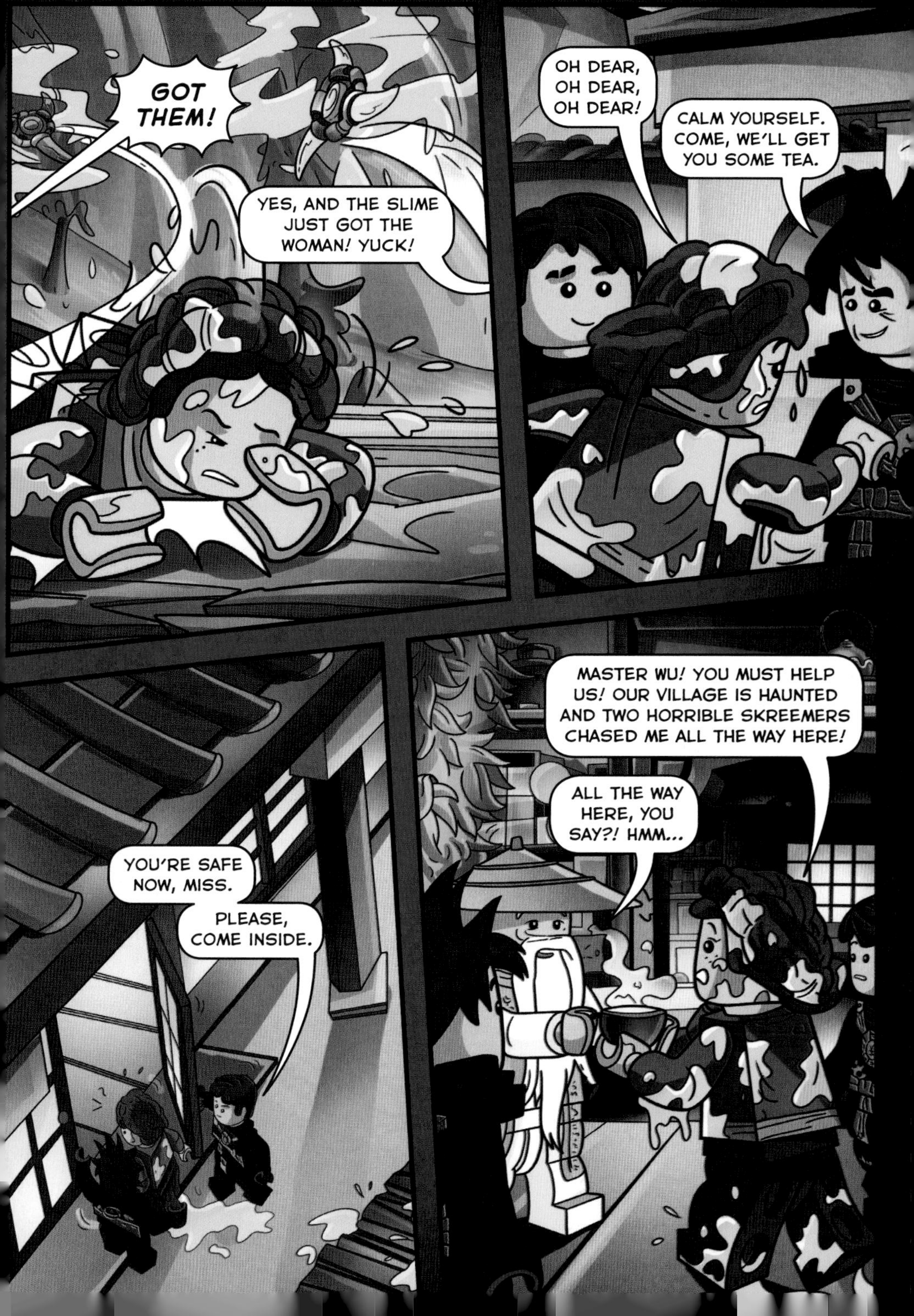
GOT THEM!
YES, AND THE SLIME JUST GOT THE WOMAN! YUCK!
OH DEAR, OH DEAR, OH DEAR!
CALM YOURSELF. COME, WE'LL GET YOU SOME TEA.
YOU'RE SAFE NOW, MISS.
PLEASE, COME INSIDE.
MASTER WU! YOU MUST HELP US! OUR VILLAGE IS HAUNTED AND TWO HORRIBLE SKREEMERS CHASED ME ALL THE WAY HERE!
ALL THE WAY HERE, YOU SAY?! HMM...

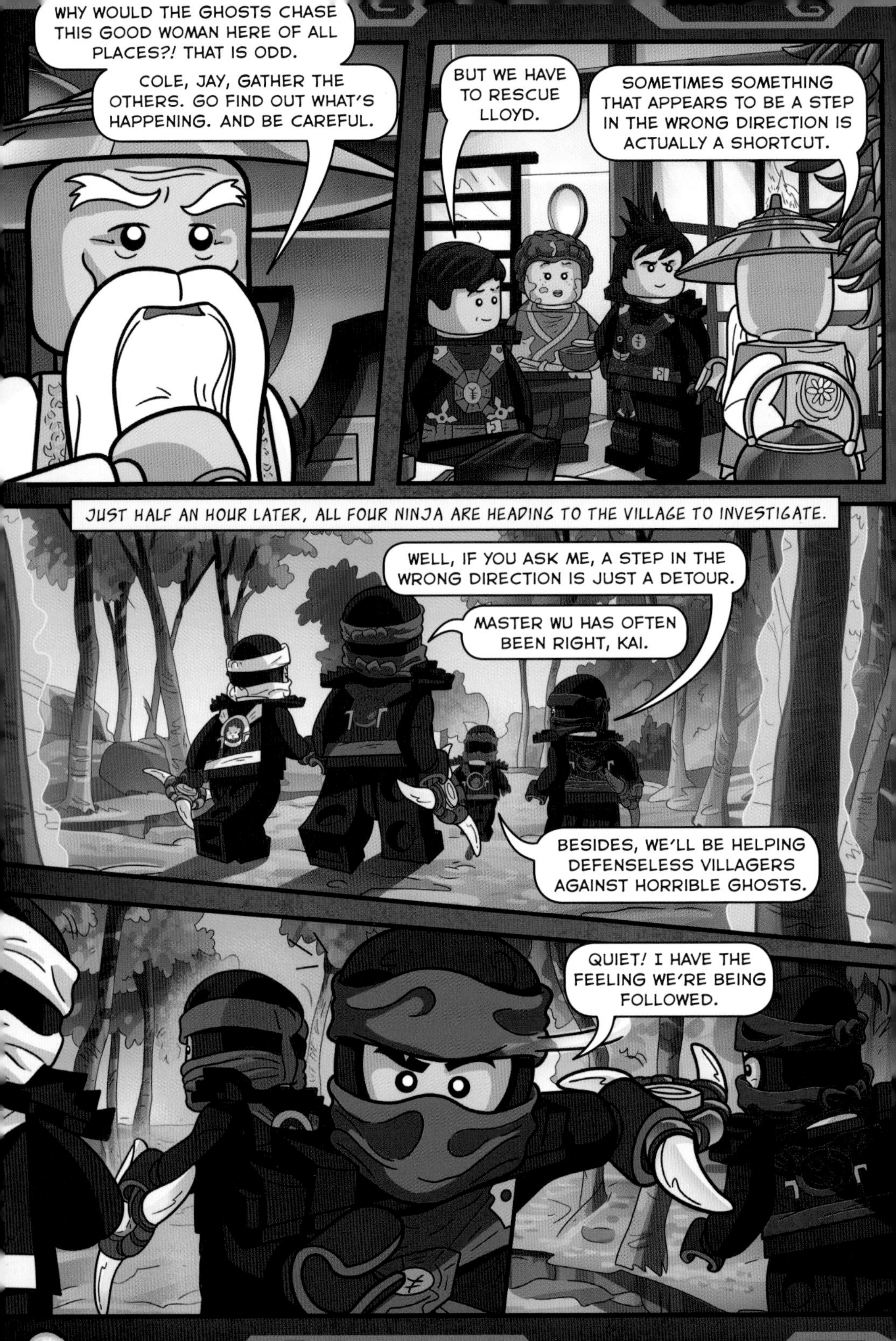
WHY WOULD THE GHOSTS CHASE THIS GOOD WOMAN HERE OF ALL PLACES?! THAT IS ODD.
COLE, JAY, GATHER THE OTHERS. GO FIND OUT WHAT'S HAPPENING. AND BE CAREFUL.
BUT WE HAVE TO RESCUE LLOYD.
SOMETIMES SOMETHING THAT APPEARS TO BE A STEP IN THE WRONG DIRECTION IS ACTUALLY A SHORTCUT.
JUST HALF AN HOUR LATER, ALL FOUR NINJA ARE HEADING TO THE VILLAGE TO INVESTIGATE.
WELL, IF YOU ASK ME, A STEP IN THE WRONG DIRECTION IS JUST A DETOUR.
MASTER WU HAS OFTEN BEEN RIGHT, KAI.
BESIDES, WE'LL BE HELPING DEFENSELESS VILLAGERS AGAINST HORRIBLE GHOSTS.
QUIET! I HAVE THE FEELING WE'RE BEING FOLLOWED.

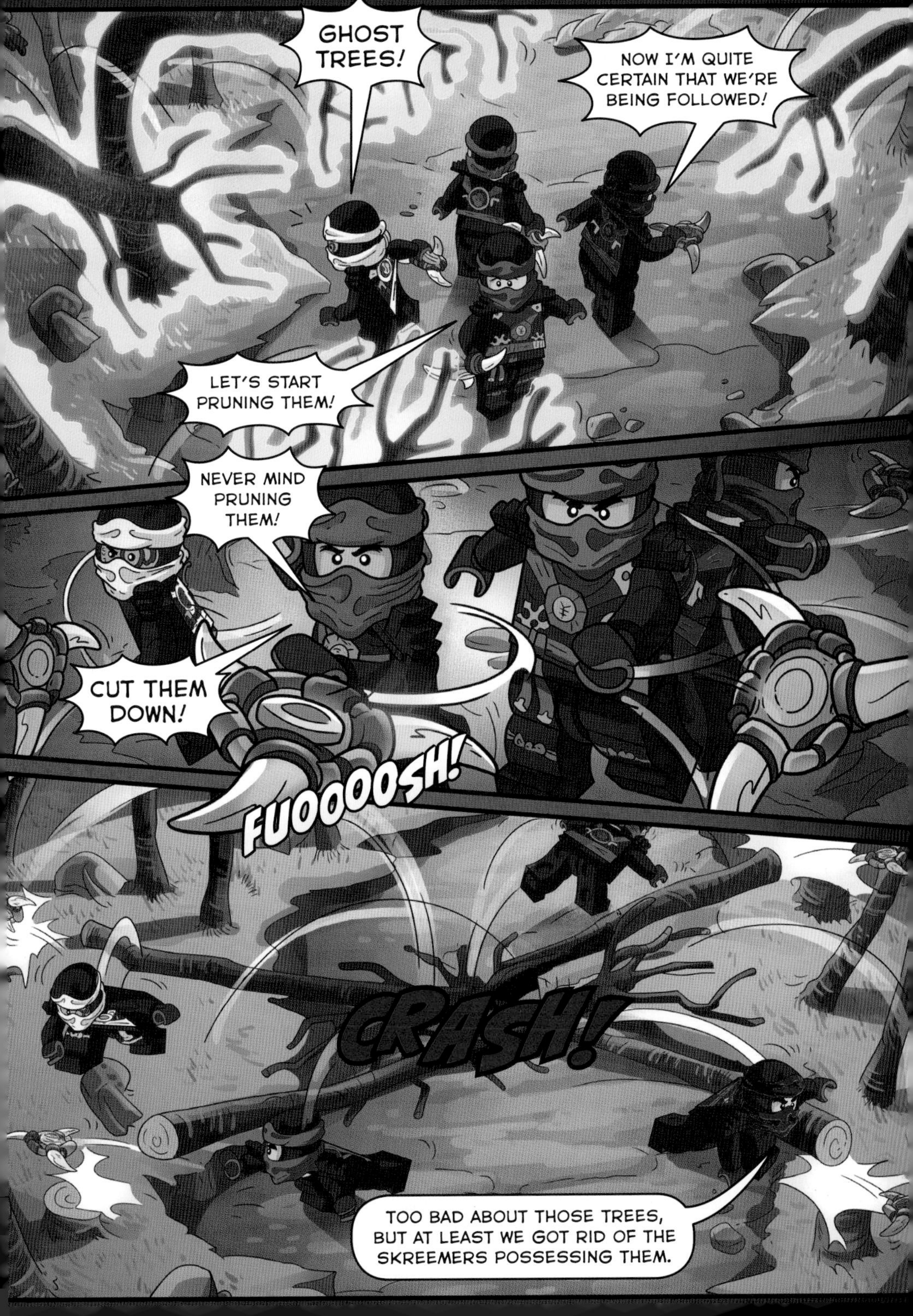
GHOST TREES!
NOW I'M QUITE CERTAIN THAT WE'RE BEING FOLLOWED!
LET'S START PRUNING THEM!
NEVER MIND PRUNING THEM!
CUT THEM DOWN!
FUOOOOSH!
CRASH!
TOO BAD ABOUT THOSE TREES, BUT AT LEAST WE GOT RID OF THE SKREEMERS POSSESSING THEM.

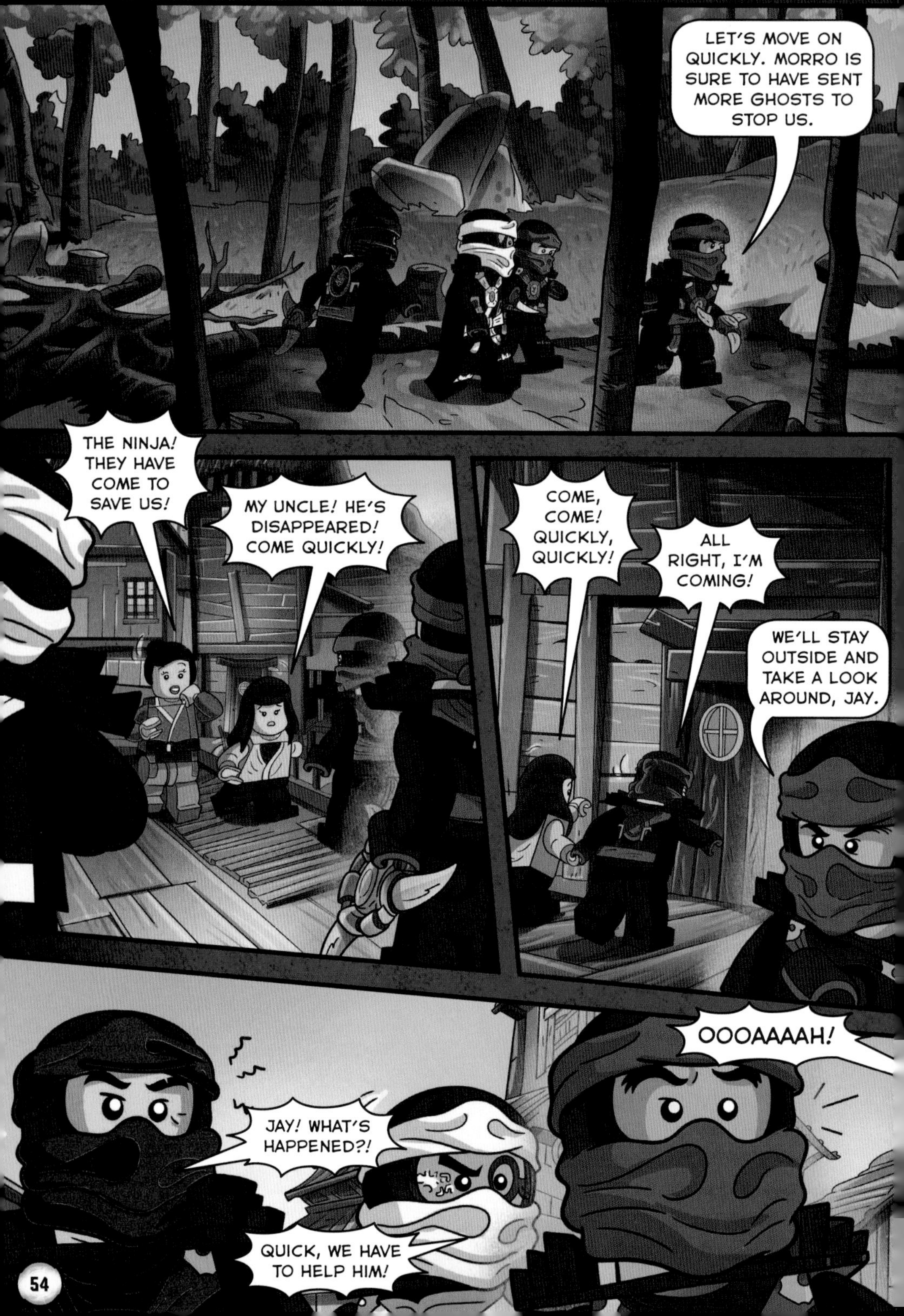
LET'S MOVE ON QUICKLY. MORRO IS SURE TO HAVE SENT MORE GHOSTS TO STOP US.
THE NINJA! THEY HAVE COME TO SAVE US!
MY UNCLE! HE'S DISAPPEARED! COME QUICKLY!
COME, COME! QUICKLY, QUICKLY!
ALL RIGHT, I'M COMING!
WE'LL STAY OUTSIDE AND TAKE A LOOK AROUND, JAY.
OOOAAAAH!
JAY! WHAT'S HAPPENED?!
QUICK, WE HAVE TO HELP HIM!

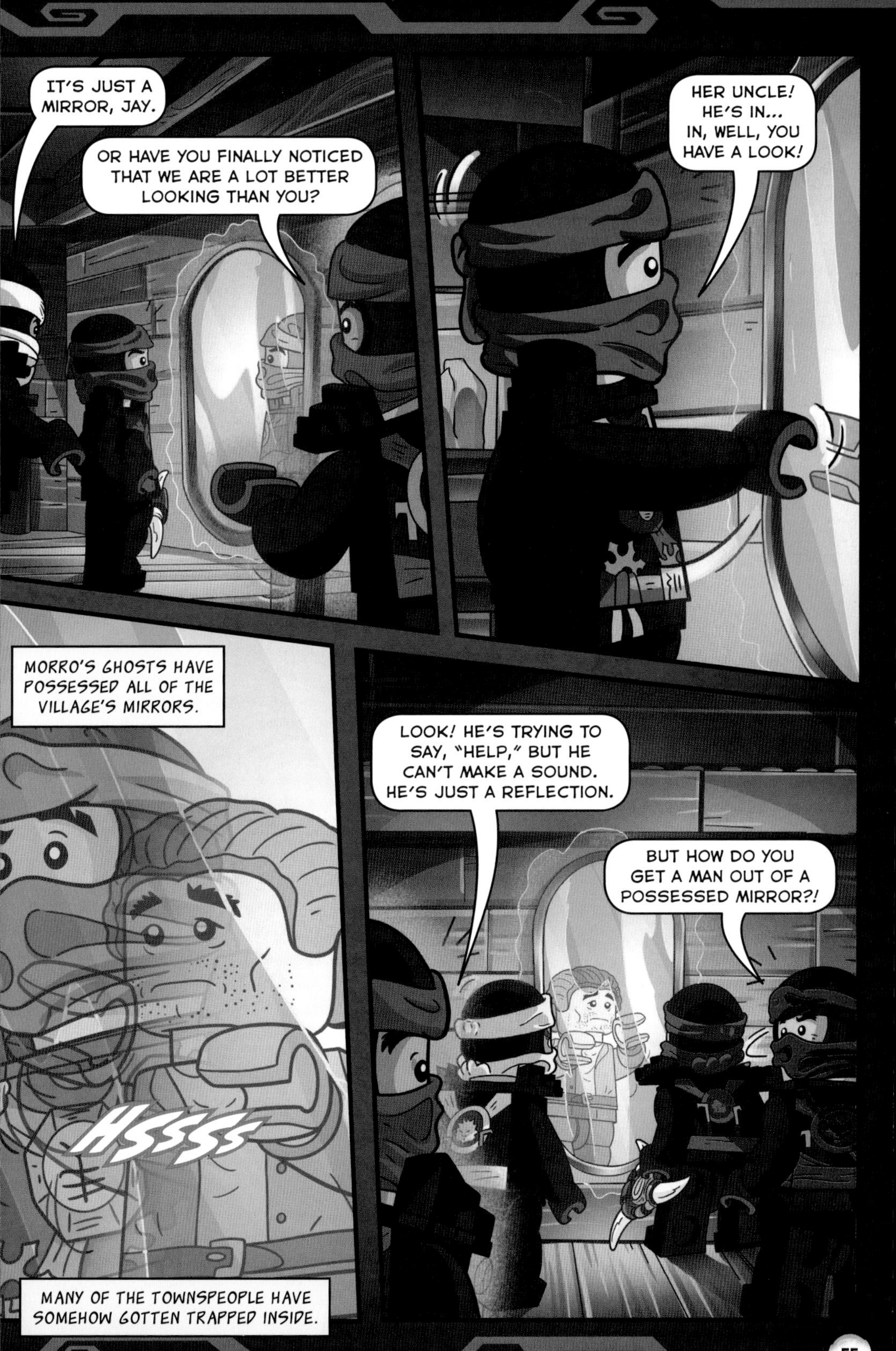
IT'S JUST A MIRROR, JAY.
OR HAVE YOU FINALLY NOTICED THAT WE ARE A LOT BETTER LOOKING THAN YOU?
HER UNCLE! HE'S IN... IN, WELL, YOU HAVE A LOOK!
MORRO'S GHOSTS HAVE POSSESSED ALL OF THE VILLAGE'S MIRRORS.
HSSSS
MANY OF THE TOWNSPEOPLE HAVE SOMEHOW GOTTEN TRAPPED INSIDE.
LOOK! HE'S TRYING TO SAY, "HELP," BUT HE CAN'T MAKE A SOUND. HE'S JUST A REFLECTION.
BUT HOW DO YOU GET A MAN OUT OF A POSSESSED MIRROR?!

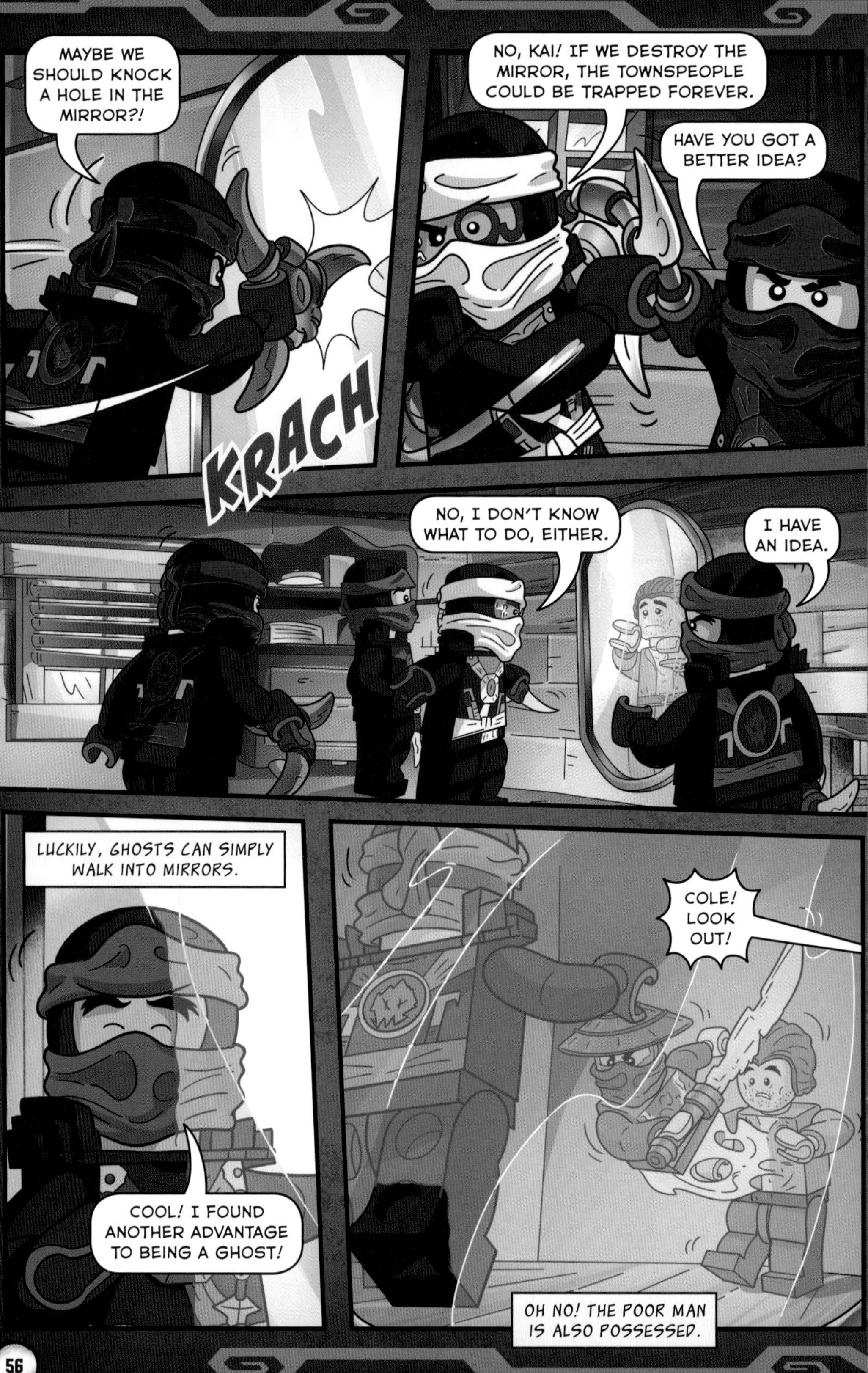
MAYBE WE SHOULD KNOCK A HOLE IN THE MIRROR?!
KRACH
NO, KAI! IF WE DESTROY THE MIRROR, THE TOWNSPEOPLE COULD BE TRAPPED FOREVER.
HAVE YOU GOT A BETTER IDEA?
NO, I DON'T KNOW WHAT TO DO, EITHER.
I HAVE AN IDEA.
LUCKILY, GHOSTS CAN SIMPLY WALK INTO MIRRORS.
COOL! I FOUND ANOTHER ADVANTAGE TO BEING A GHOST!
COLE! LOOK OUT!
OH NO! THE POOR MAN IS ALSO POSSESSED.

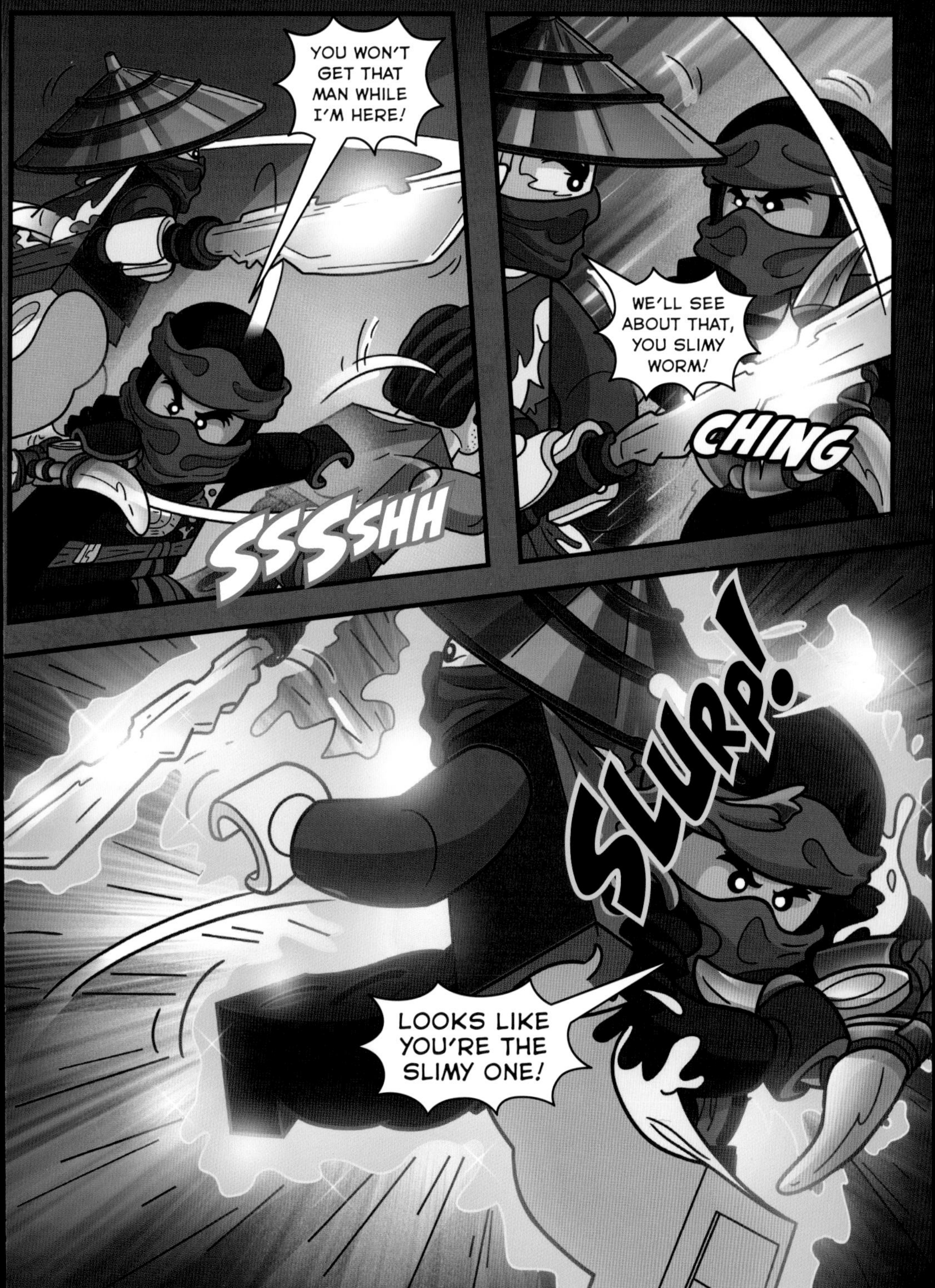
YOU WON'T GET THAT MAN WHILE I'M HERE!
SSSSHH
WE'LL SEE ABOUT THAT, YOU SLIMY WORM!
CHING
SLURP!
LOOKS LIKE YOU'RE THE SLIMY ONE!

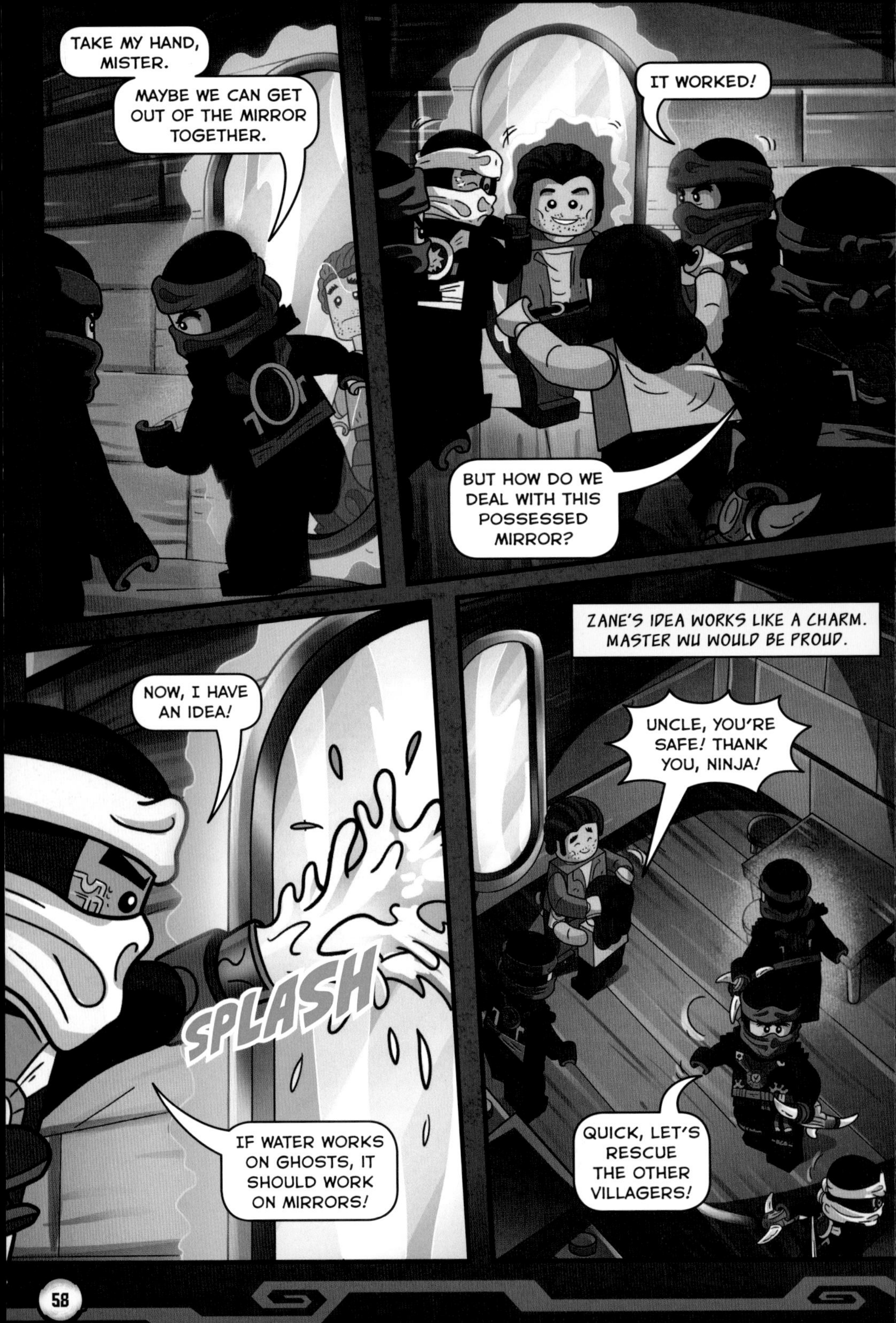
TAKE MY HAND, MISTER.
MAYBE WE CAN GET OUT OF THE MIRROR TOGETHER.
IT WORKED!
BUT HOW DO WE DEAL WITH THIS POSSESSED MIRROR?
NOW, I HAVE AN IDEA!
SPLASH
IF WATER WORKS ON GHOSTS, IT SHOULD WORK ON MIRRORS!
ZANE'S IDEA WORKS LIKE A CHARM. MASTER WU WOULD BE PROUD.
UNCLE, YOU'RE SAFE! THANK YOU, NINJA!
QUICK, LET'S RESCUE THE OTHER VILLAGERS!

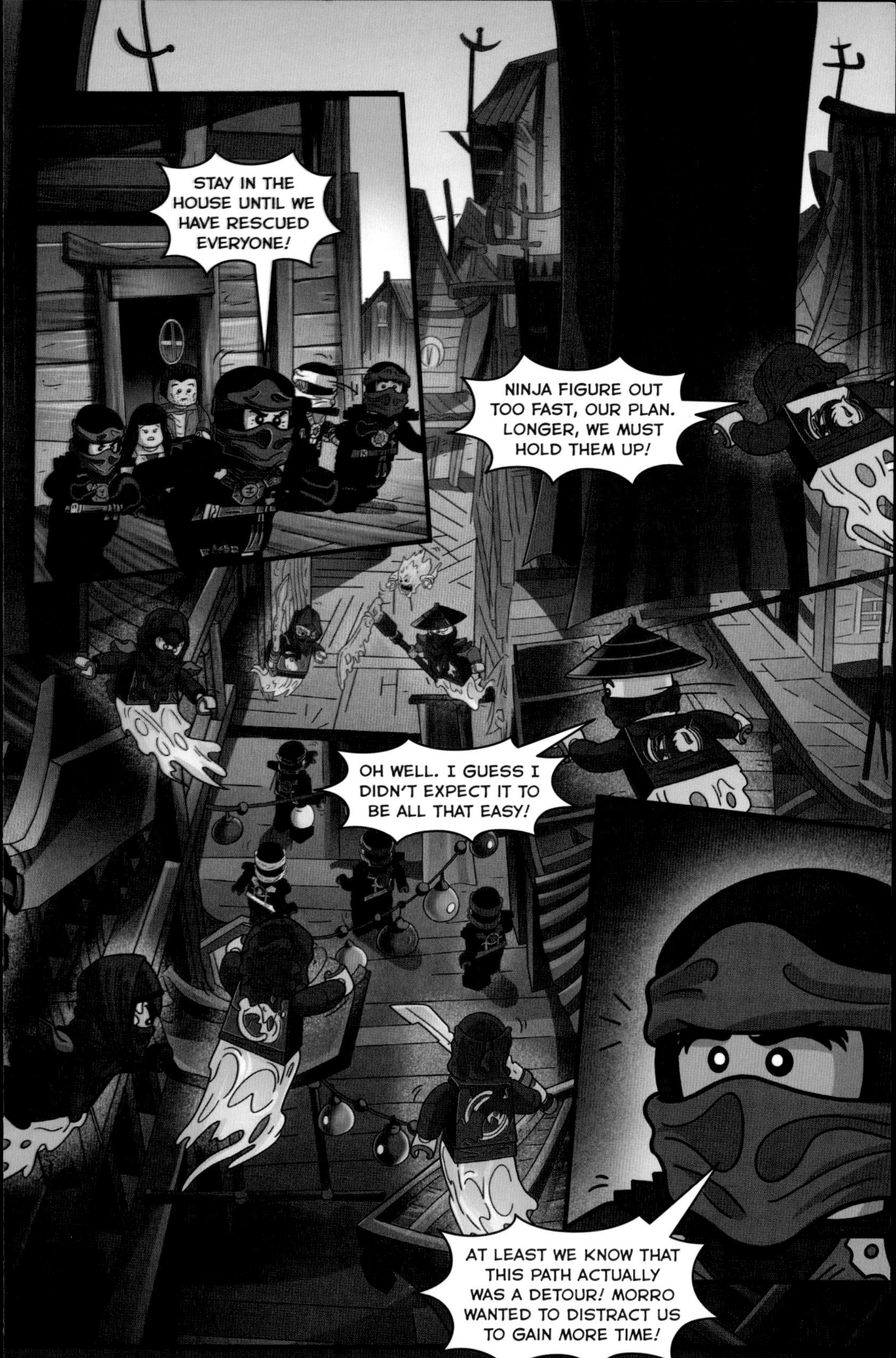
STAY IN THE HOUSE UNTIL WE HAVE RESCUED EVERYONE!
NINJA FIGURE OUT TOO FAST, OUR PLAN. LONGER, WE MUST HOLD THEM UP!
OH WELL. I GUESS I DIDN'T EXPECT IT TO BE ALL THAT EASY!
AT LEAST WE KNOW THAT THIS PATH ACTUALLY WAS A DETOUR! MORRO WANTED TO DISTRACT US TO GAIN MORE TIME!

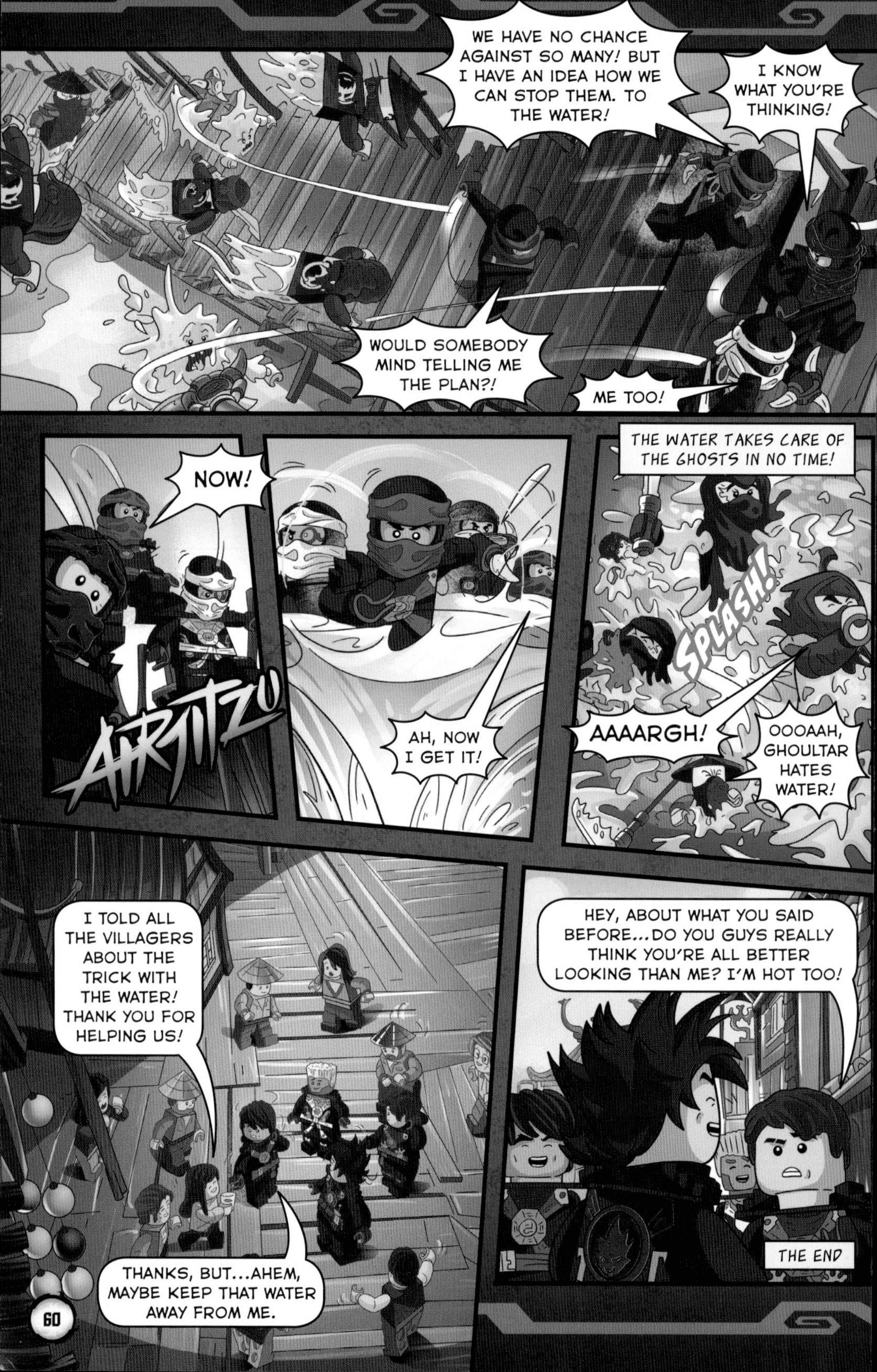
WE HAVE NO CHANCE AGAINST SO MANY! BUT I HAVE AN IDEA HOW WE CAN STOP THEM. TO THE WATER!
I KNOW WHAT YOU'RE THINKING!
WOULD SOMEBODY MIND TELLING ME THE PLAN?!
ME TOO!
NOW!
AIRJITZU
AH, NOW I GET IT!
THE WATER TAKES CARE OF THE GHOSTS IN NO TIME!
SPLASH!
AAAARGH!
OOOAAH, GHOULTAR HATES WATER!
I TOLD ALL THE VILLAGERS ABOUT THE TRICK WITH THE WATER! THANK YOU FOR HELPING US!
THANKS, BUT...AHEM, MAYBE KEEP THAT WATER AWAY FROM ME.
HEY, ABOUT WHAT YOU SAID BEFORE...DO YOU GUYS REALLY THINK YOU'RE ALL BETTER LOOKING THAN ME? I'M HOT TOO!
THE END

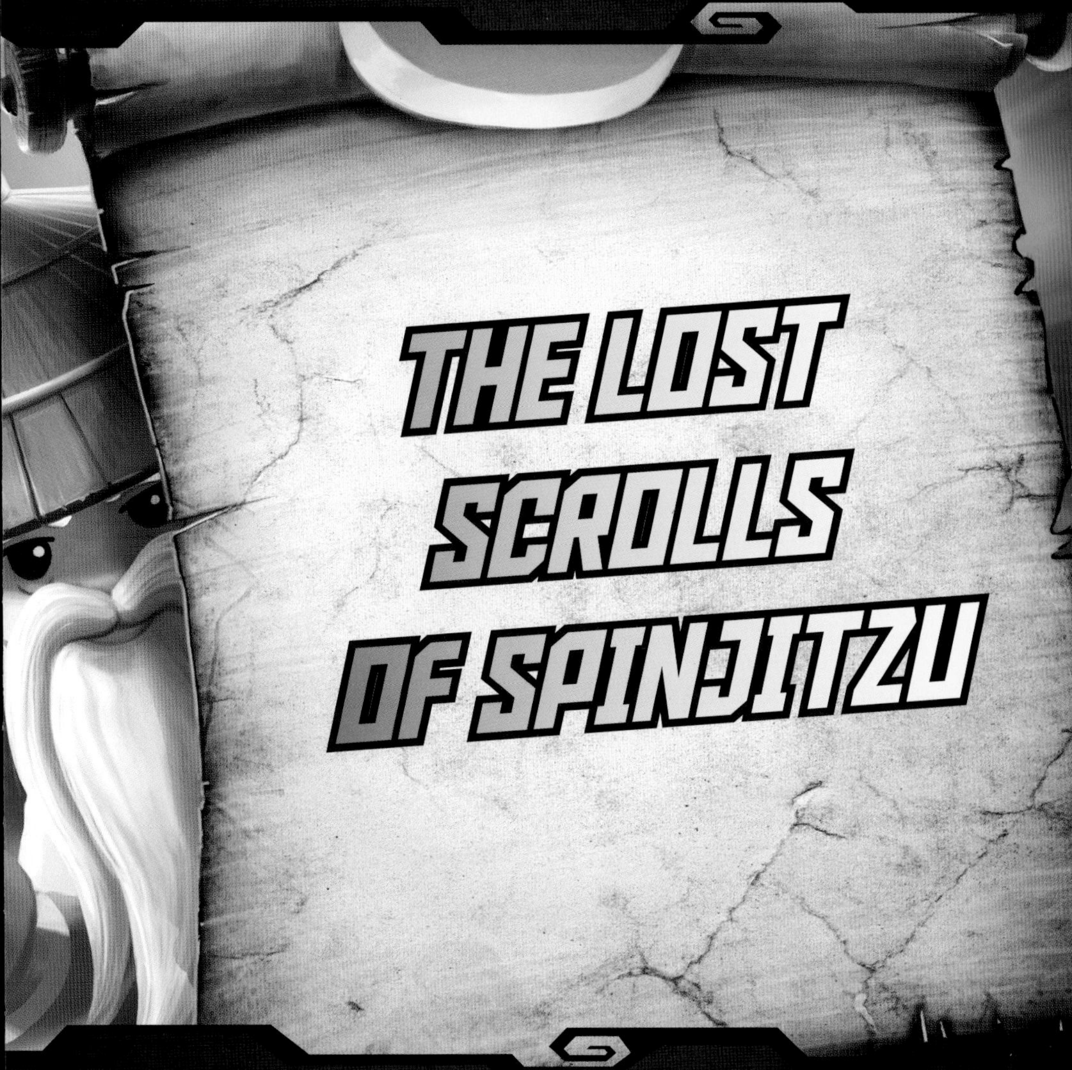
THE LOST
SCROLLS
OF SPINJITZU

Welcome to the Ninjago World

The Ninjago world was created long ago by the First Spinjitzu Master using the power of the Golden Weapons. Although this realm was initially a place of peace and light, evil arose in the person of the Overlord, who wished dominion over the planet. With no end to the struggle in sight, the First Spinjitzu Master took the drastic step of splitting the land of Ninjago in half. The

Overlord and his followers were trapped on a portion that came to be known as the Island of Darkness.

This was not the end of threats to the planet. The first Serpentine War pitted humans against snake warriors. One of the First Spinjitzu Master's sons, Garmadon, was corrupted by

darkness and tried to conquer the world, only to be defeated by his brother, Wu. Master Wu would go on to defend the planet against various menaces for years to come, before eventually recruiting a team of young ninja to help him.

Ninjago is a geographically diverse planet, with volcanoes, deserts, ice caps, dense forests and jungles, toxic bogs, and more. Only one city is known to exist, Ninjago City, but there are long-lost cities dotting the

landscape. There are also a large number of villages and farming communities.

The ninja's adventures have carried them all over the planet, and they have saved the Ninjago world many times over. Time will tell what excitement the future has in store for them!

Ninjago map

1. Golden Peaks
2. Master Chen's Island
3. Ninjago City
4. Anacondrai Tomb
5. Samurai X Cave
6. Steap Wisdom Tea Farm
7. Kryptarium Prison
8. Hiroshi's Labyrinth
9. Tomb of the First Spinjitzu Master
10. Tiger Widow Island
11. Temple of Airjitzu
12. Wailing Alps
13. Corridor of Elders
14. City of Stiix
15. Spirit Coves

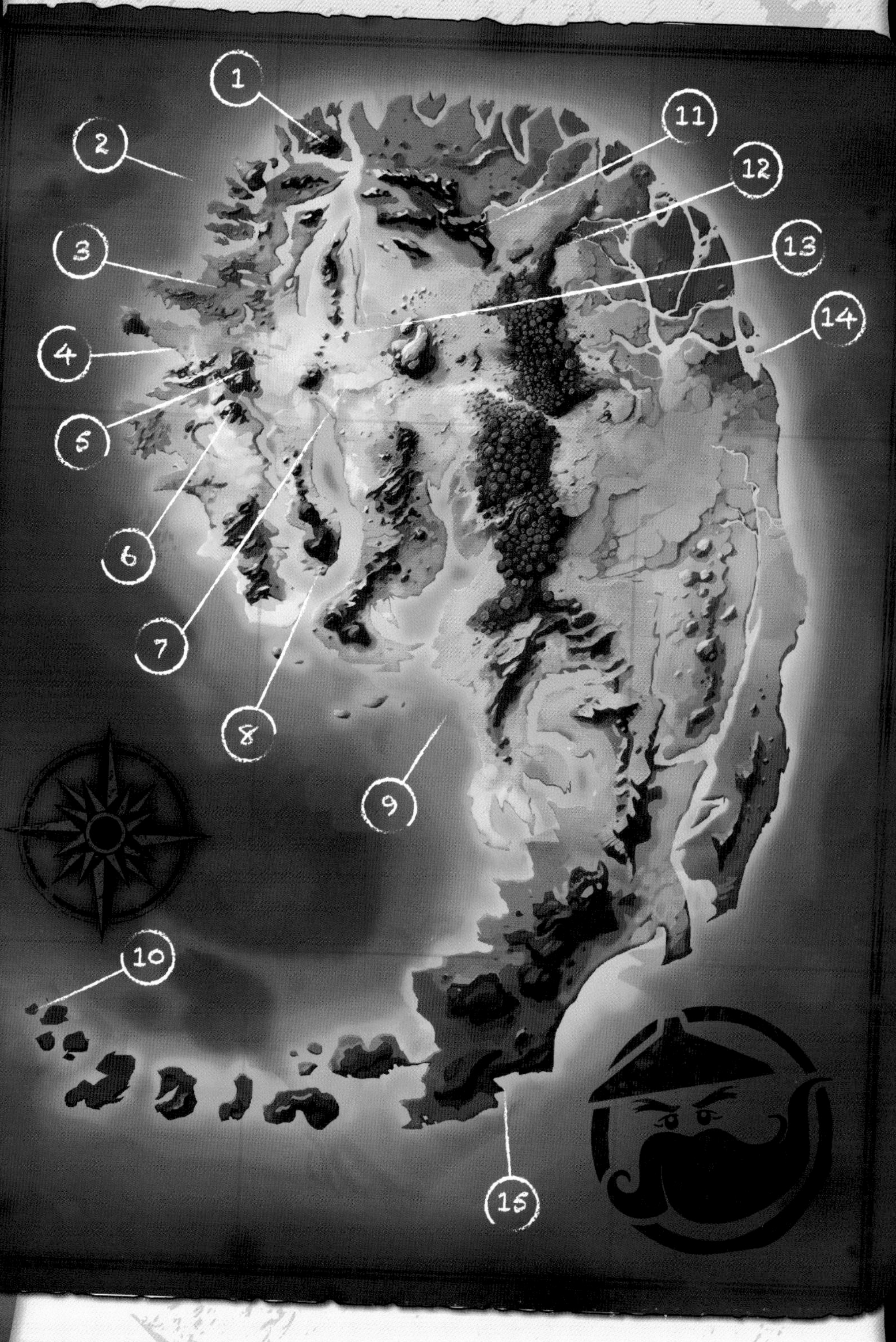
1
2
3
4
5
6
7
8
9
10
11
12
13
14
15

RONIN! HERO OR VILLAIN?

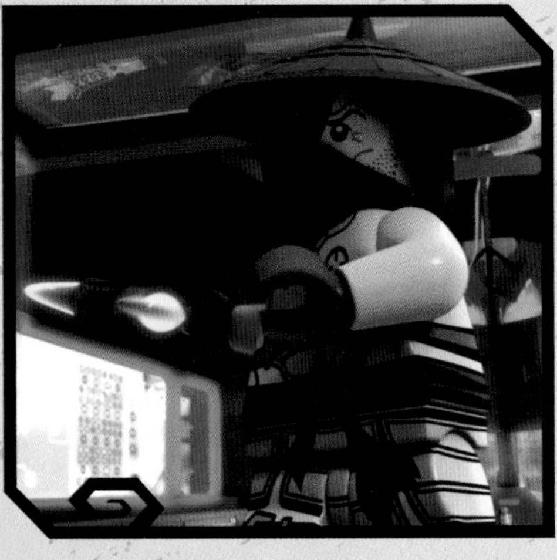

The only master Ronin serves is the almighty dollar. He's a thief who's known to have made a few bad bets—including selling his soul to the Soul Archer. When his path intersects with the ninja, Ronin has a chance to make things right and be a hero for once. But what's in it for him?

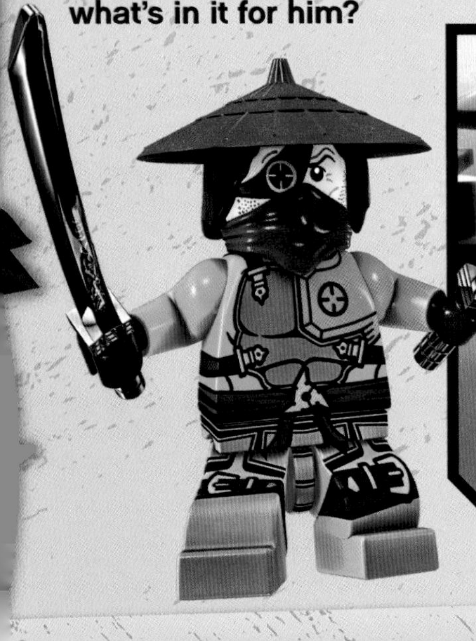

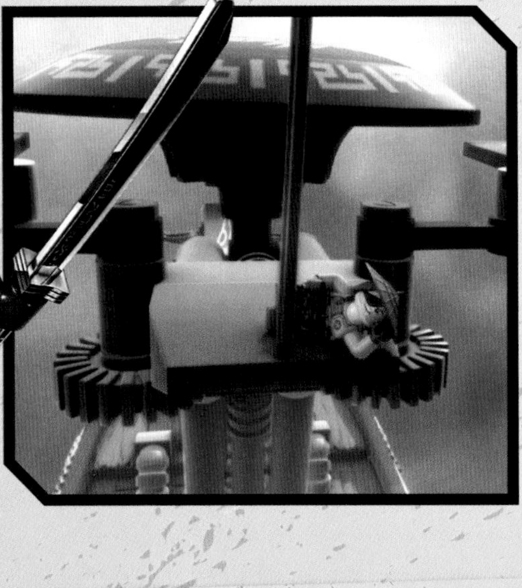

MORRO, MASTER OF WIND

Morro was Master Wu's first pupil. Long ago, after seeing his command of the wind, Wu trained him to be the Green Ninja. But there was a darkness inside Morro and a thirst to be the best, like no other. This worried Wu, and when the Golden Weapons didn't react in the Green Ninja ceremony, Wu tried to convince Morro to give up...but he wouldn't.

Wanting to prove Wu wrong, Morro went out in search of the Lost Tomb of the First Spinjitzu Master but never came back. Little did Wu realize, Morro was banished to the Cursed Realm, where he patiently waited to get a second chance to become the Green Ninja, and when Lord Garmadon opened the door while defeating Master Chen, Morro finally got his wish.

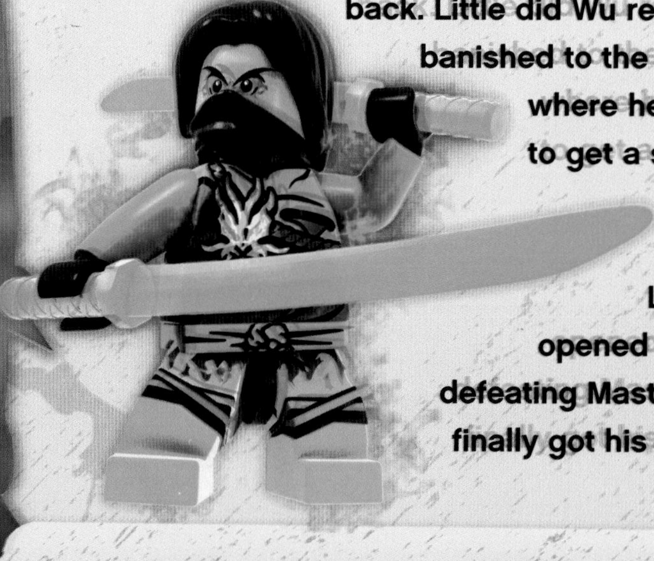

THE PREEMINENT

The Preeminent isn't just the ruler of the Cursed Realm, she IS the Cursed Realm. All encompassing, she has a primordial thirst to curse all that she touches. That means

she won't be satisfied with just Ninjago—she won't stop until she has devoured all sixteen realms.

SOUL ARCHER

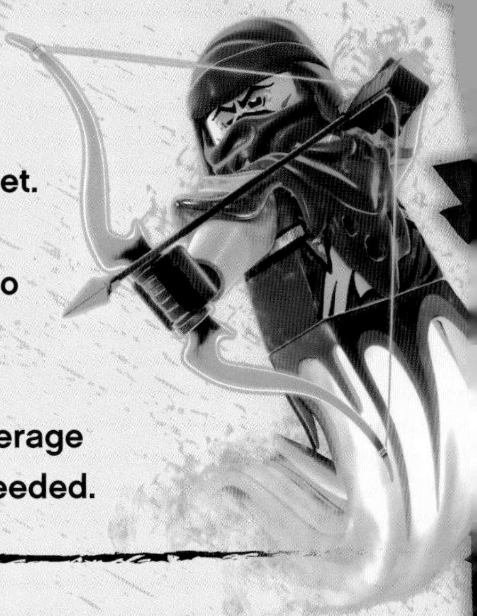

Soul Archer never misses. With his supernatural bow and arrows, he always finds his target. This Ghost Archer is Morro's right-hand man and a menace to the ninja. When he's not helping Morro, he's out there collecting souls and biding his time to leverage them to aid his evil will when needed.

BANSHA

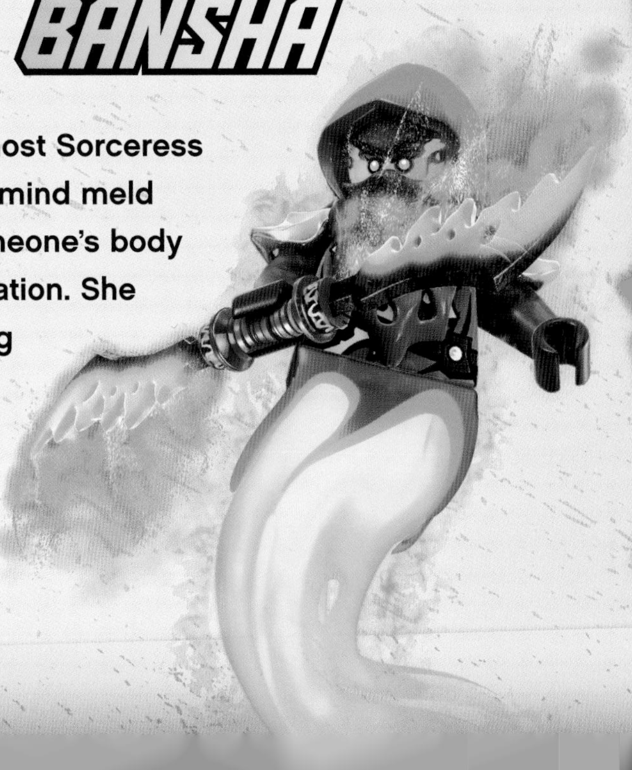

Bansha is a Ghost Sorceress with the power to mind meld and take over someone's body from a distant location. She also has a piercing scream that can shatter eardrums and cause catastrophic havoc.

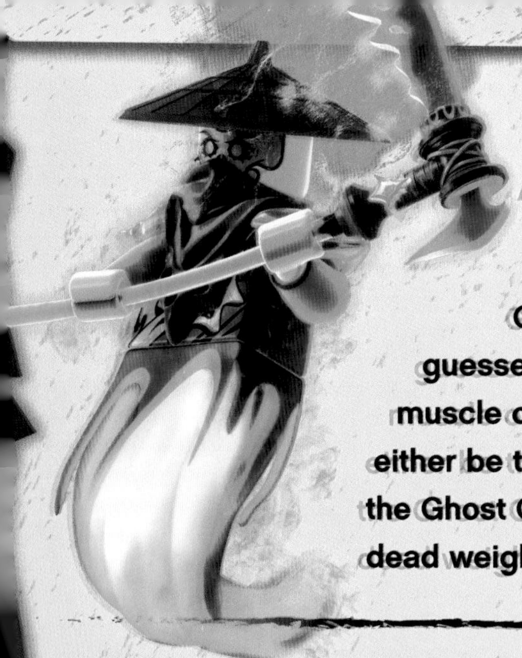

GHOULTAR

Dumb and strong, Ghoultar never second-guesses an order. As the ghost muscle of the group, Ghoultar can either be the strength needed to put the Ghost Generals over the top or the dead weight that will sink them.

WRAYTH

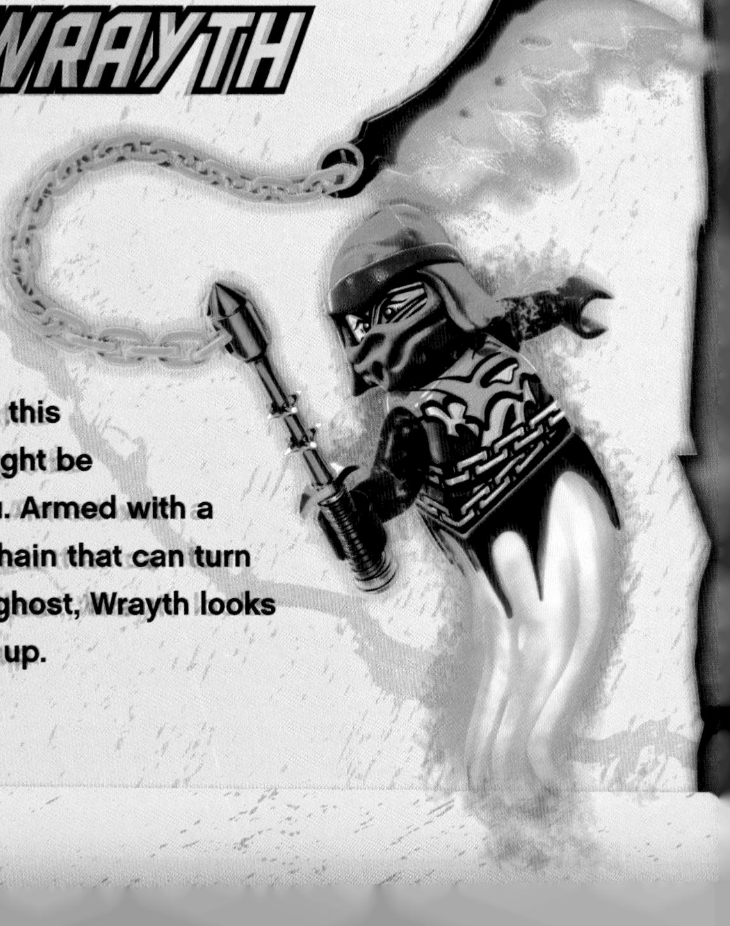

If you hear cackling and the rev of his ghost cycle, watch your back, because this Ghost Biker might be coming for you. Armed with a supernatural chain that can turn anyone into a ghost, Wrayth looks to tie the ninja up.

THE GHOST NINJA

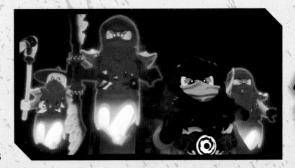

The ninja have battled their share of baddies, but these ghosts prove to be one of their biggest challenges yet. Not only can they possess nearly anyone and anything around, but the only way to stop one is with either water or weapons made of Deepstone.

DEEPSTONE AEROBLADES

Deepstone is a rare mineral mined from the bottom of the ocean. Since it's the only solid that can make contact with an ethereal ghost, what better way to use it than with an Aeroblade—a boomerang-esque weapon that returns to its master...most of the time?

AIRJITZU

An ancient martial art created by Master Yang, Airjitzu allows a Spinjitzu Master to propel himself into the air and temporarily take flight. Or as Jay likes to call it—"Cyclondo!" It's a difficult art to master but integral to the ninja's mission.

THE REALM CRYSTAL

The Realm Crystal is so powerful, the First Spinjitzu Master kept it close to him at his hidden burial site because he didn't want it to fall into the wrong hands. The crystal has sixteen sides, and if exposed to light, it will open one of sixteen portals to other worlds. Morro is after the crystal because it is the only way for the Preeminent to cross over into Ninjago.

THE SWORD OF SANCTUARY

Though it looks like a normal sword, the Sword of Sanctuary foretells an opponent's next move within the reflection of its blade. Wielded properly, it's a devastating weapon that automatically gives the carrier the upper hand in battle, but it can also help guide its wielder through impossible traps and imminent danger.

THE ALLIED ARMOR OF AZURE

If ninja find themselves in a jam and in need of some help, they might want to wear this magical breastplate. If your opponent has it—look out, because at any moment he or she can conjure the aid of allies. When Morro steals it, he's able to usher a few ghost friends from the Cursed Realm.

STEEP WISDOM

Since Wu knows so much about teas, why not open a business? Much of the ninja's operations are run out of

Master Wu's tea farm—which is good, since they are struggling to find customers. When the ninja sell their shares to Ronin in exchange for some lifesaving help, Wu gets an unexpected business partner.

THE WAILING ALPS

The Wailing Alps are the tallest peaks in Ninjago and are named after the "wailing" wind gusts that could blow one clear off the mountain if not properly tied down.

They're cold, with unrelenting blizzards. As if these peaks weren't high enough, they are merely a stepping-stone to the Cloud Kingdom.

STIIX

If there's anything that smells worse than the coast, it's the dilapidated village of Stiix, which extends over it. In constant disrepair, Stiix is a rickety cesspool of fishmongers and vagrants...which is why it's the perfect home for Ronin and his pawnshop. Eventually, Stiix becomes Morro's headquarters and the location of the Preeminent's arrival.

THE CLOUD KINGDOM

There's a kingdom in the clouds, and the denizens of this regal realm are doing more than just looking down on Ninjago—they are writing its destiny! It was they who decided Lloyd should be the Green Ninja, that Zane should be a Nindroid, and that Cole would be a ghost. But just because they have written the past, doesn't mean they always know the future. (After all, those who live in the Cloud Kingdom may know a person's destiny, but they don't always know how those who live below will arrive at it.)

THE LOST TOMB OF THE FIRST SPINJITZU MASTER

It is a place of legend, thought never to have existed. But after finding an encoded message on Master Wu's staff, the ninja discover it's real. To actually get there is another

thing entirely. First they'll need to learn Airjitzu so they can get to the Cloud Kingdom. Then they must procure the Sword of Sanctuary to see past the deadly puzzle traps protecting the jewel of the burial site—the all-powerful Realm Crystal.

THE LIBRARY IN DOMU

In this awe-inspiring place, you can find any book written on anything...ever!

Managed by monks and students of history, this location will prove a valuable source of knowledge and history. What secrets does Ninjago's mysterious past hold? You can find the answers here if you dig deep enough in the seemingly infinite collection of books.

YANG'S HAUNTED TEMPLE

There were other masters in Ninjago, and not all of them as sweet as Wu. Master Yang was hard on his students, but he is responsible for creating Airjitzu—just the coolest thing since Spinjitzu. The problem is, Master Yang is no longer around, and now his spirit haunts his temple, an architectural relic from a bygone era of Ninjago.

CAN YOU DECODE THE SECRET MESSAGE?

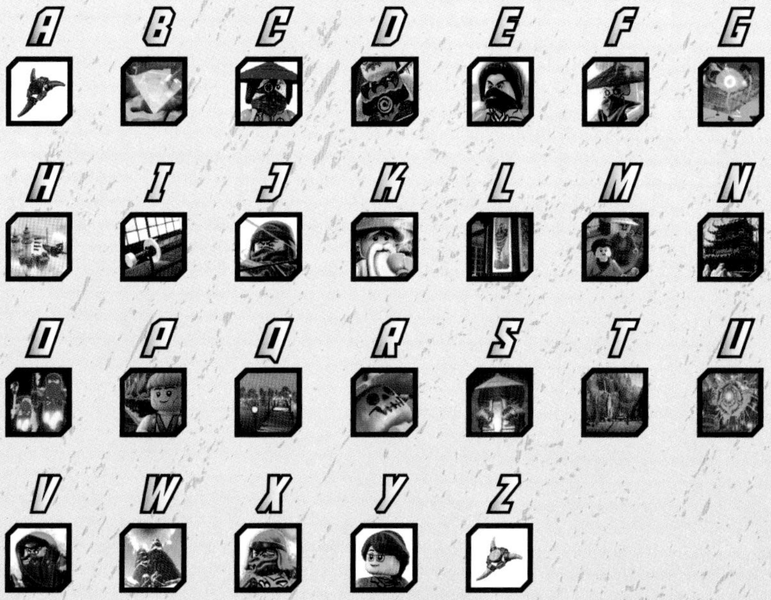
A B C D E F G
H I J K L M N
O P Q R S T U
V W X Y Z

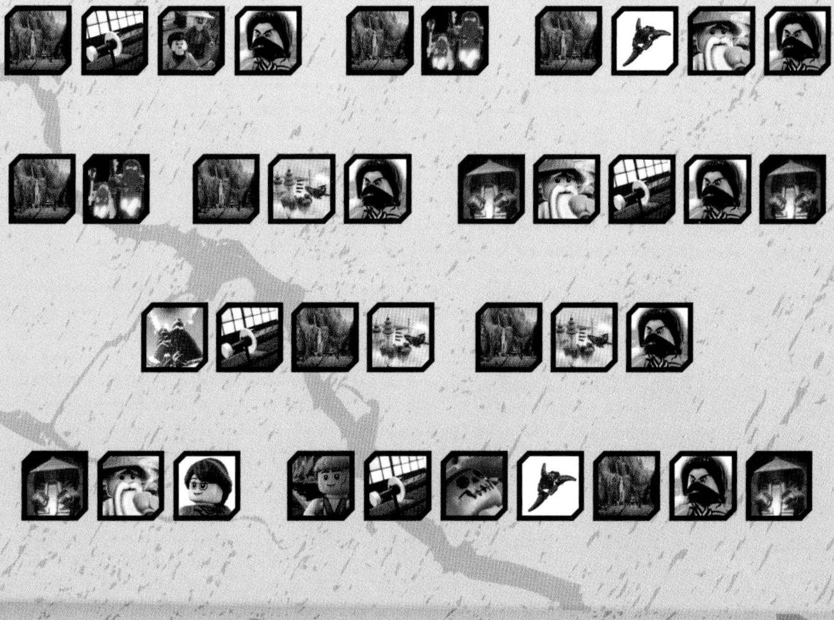

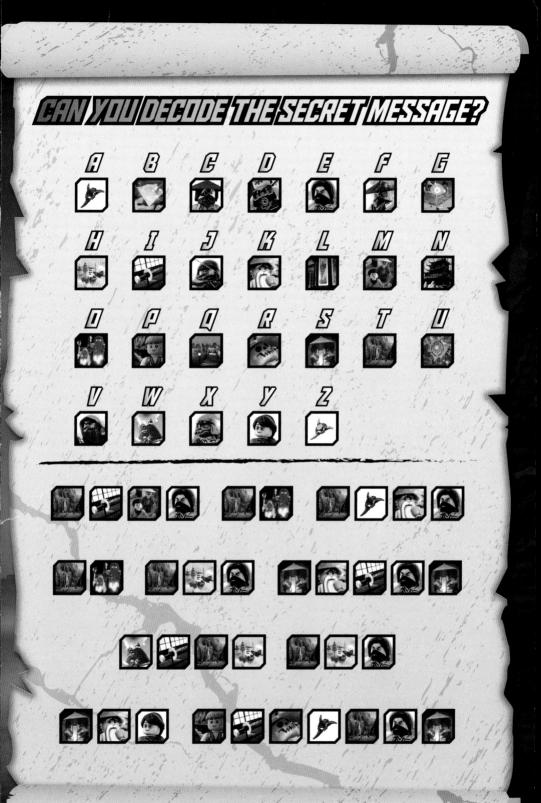

LEGO
EPIC NEW GRAPHIC NOVELS!
LEGO NINJAGO
Masters of Spinjitzu
TOURNAMENT OF ELEMENTS
BONUS PAGES!
Secrets! Codes! Maps! And more!
LEGO Friends
Adventures in Heartlake City
LEGO BIONICLE
GATHERING OF THE TOA
Also available now!
LB
LITTLE, BROWN AND COMPANY
BOOKS FOR YOUNG READERS
LEGO, the LEGO logo, NINJAGO, the NINJAGO logo, BIONICLE, the FRIENDS logo and the Minifigure are trademarks of the LEGO Group. ©2016 The LEGO Group

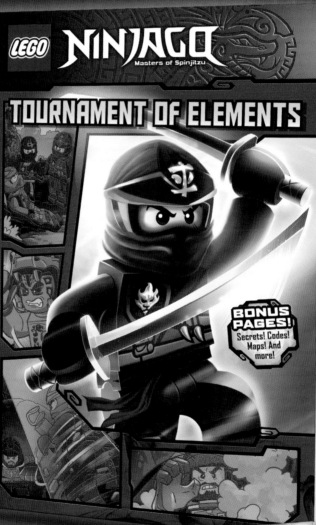

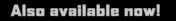